I0734554

Flirting with Paradise

ALOHA ROMANCE SERIES ~ BOOK NINE

CHRIS KENISTON

Indie House Publishing

MORE BOOKS
By Chris Keniston

Hart Land
Heather
Lily
Violet
Iris
Hyacinth
Rose
Calytrix
Zinnia
Poppy
Picture Perfect

Farraday Country
Adam
Brooks
Connor
Declan
Ethan
Finn
Grace
Hannah
Ian
Jamison
Keeping Eileen
Loving Chloe
Morgan
Neil

Honeymoon Series
Honeymoon for One
Honeymoon for Three
Honeymoon for Four
Honeymoon for Five

Aloha Romance Series:
Aloha Texas
Almost Paradise
Mai Tai Marriage
Dive Into You
Look of Love
Love by Design
Love Walks In
Shell Game
Flirting with Paradise

Surf's Up Flirts:
(Aloha Series Companions)
Shall We Dance
Love on Tap
Head Over Heels
Perfect Match
Just One Kiss
It Had to Be You
Cat's Meow

CHAPTER ONE

"Would you two get a room?" Brad Peyton couldn't even hit the John without his high school buddy Forrest John Maplewood making a move on the girl. Some things never changed. Well, except one. This girl was John's wife.

In the hallway of the tastefully refurbished Hawaiian home, Ava sprang away from her husband. Much like a teen caught making out on Lovers' Lane by a cop with a flashlight, she patted her hair and smoothed her dress, a delightful rush of pink filling her cheeks. Brad could definitely see why John grinned like an unrepentant fool. They had a good thing going.

"Billy and Angela should be here any minute. I'd better check on that lasagna." Ava slid out of her husband's grip and hurried to the kitchen.

Brad only allowed his gaze to trail Ava as long as was socially acceptable to stare at his good friend's wife. It wasn't that he had a thing for her or anything; he just wondered vaguely if there would ever be a woman in his life who made him feel the way John Maplewood looked.

Not that it mattered. At almost thirty-five years old, Brad wasn't ready to settle down. But watching John Maplewood, the master of charming and aloof, totally enraptured by one woman, made Brad question if it was time for him to reconsider. Ever since the festive wedding celebrations, with every visit to Kona, Brad expected to see their blissful union deteriorating. So far, the only conclusion he'd made was that, if he could package whatever these two had and sell it, he'd be richer than the British royal family. And happy as hell.

"Wunkel John!" From the back hall a squealing toddler came hurrying as fast as she could waddle without breaking into a trot—a cat hung precariously in her grip. The poor animal's toes barely touched the floor, scurrying like a hamster on a wheel to keep from being dragged by the cutest little girl with enormous brown eyes.

Brad found himself squatting to the child's level, a small part of him hoping she'd come share with him, even if he hadn't a clue what to do with her.

"Sorry about that." A long-haired brunette came hurrying after the little spitfire. "She spotted the cat the second we were in the kitchen door and before I could take a breath she'd nabbed Peaches and was off."

Grinning, John hunched down in front of his niece. "You like Peaches, don't you?"

The sweet-faced child bobbed her head, squeezing the furry feline more tightly. John's eyes momentarily flared with the same concern Brad had felt that the animal might lash out. When the cat merely glanced up, somewhat forlorn, John blew out a steady breath of air and gently eased her hold on the animal.

"We've tried to explain that Peaches is not a doll," Angela shook her head, and leaned over her little girl. "If you insist on carrying Peaches, you need to hold all of her in your arms."

Gently *Wunkle John* freed the feline from the little girl's near-strangling grasp and curled her into the child's arms. "See, like this."

The friendlier stance lasted all of a few seconds before a squirming cat found herself once again in a choke hold with her toes barely touching ground.

Billy looked pleadingly at his wife. Brad wasn't sure but from the doe-eyed look on the man's face, he suspected he didn't want to be the one to take the cat away from his little girl. The former Navy EOD tech could dismantle bombs but didn't want to tangle with a toddler. That a tiny little thing had a bruiser like Billy wrapped so easily around her finger teased a smile from Brad's lips.

"Time to let go, Sweetie." Angela slid the kitty away

from her daughter and with a single stroke along its back—no doubt in appreciation for not scratching the hell out of her daughter—the freed kitty darted away just as Billy whirled the laughing toddler into his arms.

The next thing Brad knew, John had zoomed in, and, passing the girl back and forth between them, the two men seemed to be playing an animated version of here comes the plane. The spray of giggles that followed siphoned every last drop of stress from Brad's body and had him grinning like the fool on the hill. That pang of doubt that had tapped in Brad's gut a moment ago thumped a little harder now. Maybe he *was* missing out.

"And this"—winning final custody of the little girl, Billy blew raspberries onto the swath of his daughter's exposed tummy—"is why I take advantage of every moment alone with my wife."

"Sounds like you're bucking for number two," John teased.

"Not a bad idea." Billy winked at his own wife who flushed several shades of rose.

Isabella scrambled from her dad's arms and, this time in a full trot, called happily after Peaches.

The picture looked pretty. But the reality, for most people, was more akin to the real housewives of some depraved city. Screaming spouses, spoiled children, and pets that peed on the expensive leather furniture. John had married into an amazing family. His newfound Kona clan were a happy anomaly, unlikely to be repeated. And certainly not by Brad. No, he reminded himself. City lights, high-stake deals, and no-strings-attached women made up his happy world. Suburban domesticity was not for him. Nieces, nephews, or otherwise.

"Just a few more minutes and we can sit down to dinner." Ava came back into the front room that doubled as a waiting area for her architectural offices and living room during non business hours. They had a small apartment upstairs, but Brad had learned on one of his earlier visits that when entertaining more than two, they took full advantage of the sprawl of the first floor.

"Need help with anything?" John snatched his wife's hand and squeezed.

At first this humble domestic side of John had taken a little getting used to for Brad. John, like Brad, had been raised in a full-on mansion with servants and every opportunity for some serious spoiling. All grown up, the man had lived in LA in a two story penthouse in a building John owned, and from what Brad remembered, he'd never seen the guy open the fridge door, never mind help with a dinner party. Somehow, John had slid easily into this cozy world of domestic middle class bliss. Brad wasn't sure why it worked so well, but he had to admit, it was one of the most welcoming homes he'd had the pleasure of visiting.

A flash of bright green and yellow frill darted past Brad from across the hall with little Isabella squealing gleefully in the wake of the cat now sporting a doll's dress.

Ava blew out an amused sigh. "Who knew when that scrawny stray adopted us she'd prove to be the most patient animal in the world."

"Apparently," The little girl's mother shook her head. "Izzy has clearly discovered the joy of motherhood. That poor cat has been dressed up, wrapped up, bottle-fed, burped…"

"Burped?" Brad asked.

"*Very* patient." John smiled.

"Yes," Ava confirmed. "Very."

John's hand fell casually on his wife's arm, but he continued to face Brad. "Didn't expect to see you in Kona so soon after your last visit. Problems with the Royal Palms?"

"As a matter of fact, it's doing so well that I just closed on another beachfront property." All it had taken for Brad to fall in love with the relaxing Hawaiian lifestyle was a single visit to Kona for John and Ava's wedding. When an opportunity to buy into a floundering hotel on the shores of Paradise landed at his feet, Brad didn't hesitate to buy the Royal Palms.

"I see." John smiled.

"Besides, I needed to work on my tan." Brad flashed his

practiced boyish grin. Experience told him it still carried an impact, even if he was far from a boy. The truth was, most of the time one of the acquisitions team would do a final walk-through to evaluate staffing before implementing changes, but this was Paradise.

Ava chuckled. By now she knew him almost as well as her husband did, and, like John, Brad was a no-nonsense businessman who hadn't worked on a tan since spring break during his college years. Truth was, he needed a breather, and Ava probably knew it.

"You can't blame the guy for not sending a grunt." Billy came in from the kitchen with a beer in one hand and an ice filled glass of water for his wife.

"Thanks, dear." Angela took the glass and shared a quick peck on the lips with the former sailor. Maybe there was something in the water on this island. Brad made a mental note to stick with beer or fruit juice on this visit.

"Whatever the reason," Ava tipped her glass of wine at him, "it's always nice to see you."

"Thanks." Spinning a coaster in his hand, he turned to face his longtime friend. "You'll get a kick out of this. Got a call yesterday from one of those reality TV shows."

"As the bachelor or will you be fawning over the bachelorette?" Except for the one hand casually rubbing the inside of his wife's palm, John remained stiff and unmoving.

"Ha, ha. Neither."

"Well it can't be Big Brother," Billy laughed.

John's eyes widened a little. "Don't tell me you're crazy enough to run around the world with a backpack or live in the jungle with only a loin cloth?"

Sputtering with reigned in amusement at his friend's assumptions, Brad set down the coaster and hefted his ankle over his knee. "The show where the head of a company goes incognito to work."

"Oh"—Angela rubbed her hands together—"I love that show. Especially the episodes when the boss makes sweeping changes that affect the whole company. Which of your companies will you infiltrate?"

"None. Apparently the former owner of Paradise Shores Hotel had agreed to participate. I have no such inclination."

"What do you mean, *no*?" Ava's brow crinkled in confusion.

"Don't look so surprised. Why the heck would I want to wear a cheap wig, thick glasses and a fake nose? I already know everything I need to. Once we replace the existing personnel with my people and fully implement my resort standards, it won't take long to turn the outdated and glorified roadside inn into a five-star destination. This walk-through is just a technicality."

"Technicality?" The tone of Ava's voice shifted to one she might use when dealing with an unusually dense underling. "The employees are people with families and bills to pay. They're more than numbers on a spreadsheet. It would do you good to see that for yourself. Besides, some of the TV show participants only need a new hairdo and—"

"Off-the-rack clothes." Brad laughed at the idea. "Like I said, no thanks. I'm not putting on a dog-and-pony show for anyone."

"You'd look good with a new nose," John deadpanned.

"Let me know when *you* go undercover, and then maybe I'll think about it." If Ava and Angela had not been in the room, Brad would have offered a different comeback. Something hitting a little further below the belt.

"I already have. Sort of." John shrugged. "Remember I spent my vacation here in Kona as regular Forrest Maplewood, not CEO John Maplewood. Besides if that doesn't count, Father had all of us work at least one summer in high school for his company. To appreciate the value of a buck. In his infinite wisdom, Ironman Maplewood decided I needed to work with the janitor."

Billy tipped his beer bottle at him. "That explains why you wield a mean mop."

"Ha ha," John teased back.

Angela shrugged at Brad "You have to admit. John's got a point about his visit here. None of us had a clue he wasn't just an ordinary construction guy."

"I think you should do it." Ava stared at Brad. "It will

be good for you and the hotel."

He could hear the dare in her tone, see it in her stare. Blast, she might not be a business mogul, but she had that don't-mess-with-me stare down pat.

"Why would I want to carve out a week or more of my already overloaded schedule? This place is no different than any other hotel we've bought out. We have a proven takeover strategy. I don't have to see the place to know what has to be done."

"It's one thing to be presented with a shiny new toy. It's another thing to be the person who shines it." Ava crossed her arms, and Brad ignored the prideful smile John bestowed on his wife.

"No," Brad repeated more sternly. The whole idea was absurd. By the time he had turned thirty, he'd bought and sold more companies than his old man had in his entire life. Brad didn't need to play doorman to evaluate the latest acquisition.

"She's right." John Maplewood was an imposing man who could get his way with just a look.

A look that didn't work on Brad. He shook his head.

A buzzer sounded from the kitchen, and Ava pushed to her feet. "Dinner will be served in ten."

"I'll go get Izzy." Angela stood and smiled at her sister-in-law. "The cat will be thrilled."

Crossing the room, Ava paused at Brad's side. "Every good CEO should know what it's like to be at the bottom of the totem pole." Then she walked away.

Shifting his gaze from his wife's departing back to his brother-in-law who merely shrugged and smiled, and finally settling on Brad, like the cocky jock he'd always been back in school, John cast a wry grin in his friend's direction. "Afraid you can't cut it?"

"That look doesn't work on me anymore."

John's grin grew. He leaned back into the leather love seat. "I dare you. No TV cameras. No gimmicks. Just you, a false name, and two weeks punching a clock."

This was ridiculous. Why was he even discussing something so absurd? All through high school, he and John had one-upped each other with dares and challenges. Stupid inconsequential things at first, like who could eat more hotdogs without barfing, but, by senior year, they'd coaxed each other into almost everything regardless of cost or risk, but that was years ago. They'd both moved on to the real world. Matured. But still, the look in John's gaze sent Brad spiraling back to their days in the hallowed halls of one of the East Coast's most elite prep school, where pissing contests seemed to be the favored pastime. There was no reason for Brad to do this. None. He had nothing to prove. To anyone.

John's smile slipped, his expression blank, his thoughts unreadable, as he leaned forward, pinning Brad with his gaze. "Unless of course, you don't think you're man enough?"

Billy burst out laughing, just as his wife and daughter walked into the room. "Oh to be a fly on the wall for this one."

Brad wasn't going to do it. There was no reason. No reason at all. Except maybe the two men glaring at him.

CHAPTER TWO

"The guests in Room 202 want you to see the hair left in the bathtub."

Hope Gibbons nodded.

"Room 215 says their trash hasn't been emptied for two days and—"

"Want me to take a look." She glanced through her scheduling charts. Lani was the housekeeper assigned to both those rooms. Damn. Hope wished it had been anyone but her. "I'll check it out."

"There's more." Nina, Hope's best housekeeper and frequent message-taker, pushed away from the desk. "The school called."

That had Hope's full attention. She had to remind herself it couldn't be serious or Nina would have tracked her down. That was a priority rule never to be broken. Nothing was more important than Jason.

"They want you to schedule your parent-teacher meeting."

Nervous anticipation whooshed out in a single breath. Short-staffed, she and just about every housekeeper at the hotel were working their asses off trying to keep up. "Thanks. I'll get back to them."

"I can cover for you."

"I don't dare. Not now." For the few months, everyone on staff had been on pins and needles since the announcement that the hotel was being sold. A few had already accepted new jobs, anticipating a heavy ax falling on the current employees. Rumor had it that, whenever EastCo Enterprises took over, out-with-the-old-and-in-with-the-new was the rule of thumb. But Hope was counting on her good record to keep this job.

"Any new word?"

Hope shook her head. According to the grapevine the official change of hands had gone down a few days ago. Now they were all just waiting for the other shoe to drop.

"Knock, knock." Keith Collier, manager of the Paradise Shores Hotel, stood in the doorway of the matchbox-size office. "Got a minute?"

"Sure."

Nina pushed to her feet. "I'd better see if anyone needs help."

Keith waited for Nina to leave as Hope held her breath. "A call came in early this morning from the new corporate office."

Hope nodded.

"Things are to continue as usual until further notice."

"Thank God." For the first time since hearing about the impending sale of the hotel, Hope breathed easy. "No more hiring freeze?"

Keith shook his head. "Not exactly."

"What do you mean?"

"Seems EastCo just did a round of hiring. We can have as many new employees as we want as soon as they're done with initial training. In the meantime, I'm getting an assistant right away."

"Oh."

"Yeah." Keith nodded.

Hope knew he'd put in a good word for Sandy and had hoped, once the transition of ownership was complete, the new owner would let Sandy step into the position of assistant manager officially. Everyone knew she'd pretty much been doing the job since the previous one had hightailed it immediately after the sale announcement.

"Does she know yet?"

Keith nodded.

A long silence hung in the air, and Hope braced herself, knowing what was coming next.

"Listen, I know you're working really hard, and Jason keeps you pretty busy, but the invitation to grab a bite one night still holds and—"

"Thanks, Keith. I appreciate it." She didn't know what else to say. Keith was a nice guy, but she just wasn't interested. Every time he asked her out, she had the same answer. He deserved a nice girl who liked him as much as he liked her, and she wasn't it.

It took him a few seconds of nodding to straighten to his full height and turn away.

Some days she wondered if she shouldn't just say yes and see what happened. There were worse things in life than dating and marrying a nice guy. Plus she did worry about Jason growing older without a strong male influence. But her son was only eight. She didn't have to have all the answers today. For now, even one new housekeeper and a supply attendant would make her day.

Not for the first time since picking up the cheap rental car had Brad thought this might very well be the worst idea he—or John—had ever had. After only a few minutes in morning traffic, he already desperately missed the sleek convertible he'd had shipped to the islands after his last business trip. Blast John Maplewood. A single challenge and, the next thing Brad knew, he'd instructed his staff to arrange for him to work at the Paradise Shores Resort as a new management trainee. He wouldn't be getting his hands dirty the way Ava wanted, but at least none of the hotel employees would be aware to suck up to the CEO of EastCo.

Nestled in a surprisingly long strip of beachfront real estate and well hidden behind a dense wall of palm trees and flora, his latest acquisition was in the perfect spot to install a luxury resort. Searching for an available employee parking space, Brad headed to the rear of the lot and parked against the wall. As CEO, he'd have an assigned space in front. As management trainee, he was going to get some exercise. Walking, he surveyed the property. The place was in better shape than he would have expected from the initial acquisition reports he'd received. Yeah, a few spots needed some attention—some cracks in the drive, some fresh paint here or there, but, overall, the grounds were well-maintained and the stuccoed Spanish architecture fit in surprisingly well with the Big Island beach scene.

Inside the lobby was spacious, bright, and even the outdated palm-tree-upholstered furnishings somehow seemed to suit the idea of a beach retreat. He was impressed. The same furnishings in a much different surrounding could have been a total turnoff. The moment the woman at the front desk met his gaze, she smiled and held his attention. Good. Whoever she was, he'd make sure she was staying.

"May I help you?" asked the blonde with the name tag that read Sandy.

"I'm here to see Keith Collier. I'm the new trainee."

For a brief flash her smile faltered before she regained her perfect posture. "Of course. One moment and I'll get him."

The bustle of early morning checkout had begun. Luggage accumulated at the front door. Outside, in the circle drive, taxis and shuttles collected their cargo. Business was doing well. Better than what he'd expected.

"Bradford Kane?" The hotel manager extended his hand.

It was too risky to use his last name, but keeping his first name and using his mother's maiden name would make completing this farce somewhat easier. "Yes. Please call me Brad." A firm but brief shake. He was beginning to like what he saw.

"Keith Collier. Today's going to be a bit of a training challenge. We are sold out for the night. My regularly scheduled registration clerk called in sick, and we're short-staffed in housekeeping as well. I'm afraid this is one of those days when everyone chips in. I'll try not to throw you to the wolves, but we don't have a lot of time for showing you the ropes." Before Brad could respond, his new supervisor took off at a brisk pace. "We'll do a quick walking tour. I'll introduce you to everyone."

"Sounds like a plan." From the lobby Brad followed the younger-than-expected manager around like a heeler hound, taking in every word. Keith seemed to know his staff by name and appeared to be well-respected—or at least liked. But then again, Brad knew from experience, appearances could be deceiving. So far he'd met the head of security and had a quick glance at the surveillance systems. The head of maintenance spoke in broken English, and Brad was surprised when Keith replied in passable Spanish. The groundskeepers took a second to nod and mumble "Okay" to Keith's instructions and quickly returned to work.

"We have a good crew here. Most people have been with us for years. It was a bit of a shock to learn the hotel was being sold."

Judging by the tic in Keith's jaw, *a shock* may have been putting it mildly. Back inside the labyrinth of oceanside rooms, they wound their way into a rear closet that turned out to be housekeeping's main office.

"This is Hope Gibbons, our head housekeeper."

From the doorway he could see a mop of dirty-blonde hair piled atop a head bowed over a desk covered in paperwork and cradling a telephone between her shoulder and one ear.

"I see. Yes. Okay." The phone landed in the cradle, and the blonde mop lifted to expose a porcelain-like face with two bright-green button eyes peering up at him with exhaustion. Those striking eyes homed in on her boss. "That was Sandy. The Red Hat group called to say their flight plans changed. They'll be arriving before check-in time and asked if we can possibly have their rooms ready by one."

"How many rooms?" Keith asked.

"Thirty."

"The airlines accommodated that many people early?"

"Charter flight." Pinching the bridge of her nose for one second, Green Eyes blinked, then focused once again on her boss. "They requested to be in a single building on the same floor. I've got an update on the few rooms vacated and waiting to be cleaned. Two of the rooms on that floor are frequent-vacationer members and have extended their check-out time. Lani called in sick. Again. I'll do my best."

Keith nodded. "Thanks. This is Brad Kane, the new management trainee."

"Nice to meet you." Hope nodded but turned to grab a clipboard.

An unexpected pang of regret over missing a chance to shake her hand caught him off guard. Nice, and pretty enough, Hope was not his usual fare. He leaned more toward long legs in high heels than the girl next door in flats. If anyone had wholesome written all over her, it was this lady. And those eyes… "Anything I can do to help?" he asked, forgetting it wasn't within his immediate power to do much.

"Any good at making beds?" She chuckled, gripping the paperwork and pen close to her chest.

"As a matter of fact—no." Even in college both his and his room mates' parents had paid for weekly maid service. The rest of the time no one bothered to make beds. "But I'm a fast learner."

Hope raised a brow at Keith, and Brad glanced over his shoulder in time to see the manager shrug in response. Hope smiled, pushed to her feet, and, turning to face him, stuck her arm straight out to shake. "Bedmaking 101 coming right up."

CHAPTER THREE

C lipboard in hand, Hope marched out the door, gladly accepting any help she could get. Taking the corner at a quick clip, she came to a halt in a storage room. "Here's the plan," she instructed the new guy. "Sheets are on those shelves there. Towels to the left. Extra pillows, top shelf. This"—she pointed to the mobile stock cart—"needs to be filled with extra sheets, towels, and toiletries. I'll fill up the housekeeping cart. You stock this one." She waited for Brad to cast a quick look around the room before nodding.

"Shall I assume heavier on the towels?" He already had a stack of sheets in hand and was shifting them to the cart.

"Exactly. Maids run through towels faster than sheets when cleaning up. A room could have one guest, but he or she may be a towel hog."

Mid-transfer Brad paused and lifted his gaze to meet hers. "Towel hog?"

"You know, one towel for the waist, one for around the shoulders, maybe another for the hair, and still another on the floor or to shave or Lord-knows-what." She grabbed a basketful of travel-size shampoos and conditioners. "Don't forget toilet paper."

Brad nodded and kept stacking.

She hadn't expected him to step up so easily. Standing tall at over six foot, with a deep tan that screamed fun in the sun and chiseled features that most cover models would kill for, Hope's initial impression of the new trainee had been *all good looks and no substance.* So far he was proving her only half right.

Both carts fully stocked, he straightened to an

impressive height. "Now what?"

"Follow me. We'll start on the floor with the Red Hat ladies."

"That's a lot of trouble to go through when check-in time is clearly stated as three o'clock."

There was the attitude she'd expected to find under the chiseled features and bedroom eyes. "The Greater Hawaiian Islands Red Hat Society has been staying at this hotel twice a year for as long as I've worked here. I see no reason to let them down at this late stage."

"Then"—Brad nodded and a slow, easy smile slid across his face, making her stomach do a handspring—"we'd better get moving."

For a guy who didn't know much about making beds, he followed directions well. At first, she'd only let him strip the beds and stuff the sheets in the dirty linen bag while she scrubbed the bathrooms. Afterward, they'd swapped places, and she'd tended to the beds while he stocked the toiletries. When the bag of used sheets was full, Brad was tasked with carrying it to the laundry closet and shoving them down the chute. By the time they'd knocked through half a dozen rooms, Brad was in charge of stripping *and* making the beds, while Hope took care of the bathrooms.

The sound of the old-fashioned ring tone—that reminded Hope of her grandmother's rotary phone—had her pulling her cell from her apron pocket. "Hello? ... Uh-huh. Okay." Her phone slid back in place, and she faced her new helper. "Mary is on the third floor and needs restocking. Take the supply cart to the service elevator I showed you. Restock her cart. Head back to the supply room, refill your cart, then catch up with me down the hall."

"Yes, ma'am." Brad clicked his heels, saluted her, and performed a near-perfect military pivot. The urge to laugh at the unexpected response was tamped down by a surprising urge to cry. It made no sense. Those hands had never seen a hard day's work. Despite the strong shoulders under the suit jacket, she couldn't picture Brad hacking military life. He was nothing like Dave, and yet that familiar ache she had thought was long-gone rose up in her chest and threatened to rob her of whatever breath was trapped in her lungs. There was a job to do and little time to do it in. She'd closed that door of her life a long time ago and couldn't let one man's gesture send her back in time.

With an unexpected spring in his step, Brad nearly danced the cart down the hall. If anyone had told him a week ago that he'd have fun making beds, he would have committed them to a mental institution. But he was having a lot of fun. Not necessarily because of the beds but the company. At first Hope had felt the need to chatter while they worked. She'd asked Brad the basic getting-to-know-you questions, and he'd kept his answers short and simple to avoid giving away too much.

When he had mentioned being a diehard college football fan, he'd been surprised to spend the next couple of rooms discussing the Aggie's last season and the current too-big-for-his-britches quarterback. Brad and Hope had fallen into an easy working rhythm, and, for the first time, he understood what people meant when they said "companionable silence." Even if Hope wasn't exactly silent.

Sometimes she whistled, sometimes she hummed, and a few times she'd actually sung a line or two of lyrics. The one time he recognized the tune he'd been tempted to sing along.

His phone buzzed, and, unlike the earlier times when he'd ignored it, now that he was alone he answered, "Peyton."

"How's it going?"

There was no mistaking John Maplewood's voice. "Better than expected."

"Really? What have you learned?"

"To make beds." Not until the words were out of his mouth and John's rumbling laughter came through the phone did Brad realize what he'd just shared with one of his oldest friends.

"You're kidding me?" No doubt his childhood friend was thinking back on all the times Brad had razzed him about grunt work in the military.

"Your wife said to get my hands dirty."

"Interesting policy. Assigning management trainees to bedmaking."

"Not exactly. I volunteered."

This time John laughed even louder. "What have you been smoking?"

The service elevator dinged. "Is there a reason you called?"

"Yeah, Ava wants to know if you're joining us for supper at her mom's?"

"Don't know yet. Can I give you a call later?"

"Sure. Let me know when you graduate to scrubbing toilets."

"Funny, Maplewood."

"Just looking to the bright side. Looking to the bright side."

"Later." Brad disconnected the call and had to laugh to himself. He couldn't get too angry with John. This was, after all, a strange way for Brad to be spending his day. And what was even stranger was how anxious he was to get back to bedmaking with Hope.

By the time he'd completed the designated deliveries, restocked, and returned to Hope's floor, she'd knocked out three more rooms and was in the fourth, leaning across the tub, rinsing the shower walls. "How's it going?"

Hope responded with a high-pitched squeal and, still holding a nearly full glass of water, spun around and doused him with what was left in the glass. "Oh, my. I'm so sorry." She tossed aside the plastic container and grabbed a nearby towel. "You scared me."

Even though the only thing touching his wet clothing was a bulky terry-cloth towel, knowing Hope's hands directed the cleanup was wreaking havoc with his senses. Needing her to stop before he did or said something he shouldn't, he snatched her wrist. Not his smartest move.

Now he had the feel of skin on skin.

Without thinking, his thumb slid against the underside of her wrist, and he sucked in a deep breath. Almonds. And vanilla. No matter how old he grew, he was convinced he would never forget that Hope Gibbons smelled of almonds and vanilla, and how her skin was softer than satin. Still holding her arm firmly in place, he didn't move. "I can handle this myself."

Shifting from staring at the hand still manacled around her wrist, she lifted those thick dark lashes and leveled her gaze with his.

Senses already on overload spiked. He was sure she could hear his heart slamming against his chest.

"I … I'm sorry." Her gaze seemed locked with his.

"You said that already." He needed fresh, icy air. "It's okay."

"Do you have a change of clothes?" She hadn't moved.

He wished he could read minds. Those bright green eyes staring at him were filled with emotions he couldn't even begin to unravel. He shook his head instead. "'Fraid not."

"Blower."

"Excuse me?" He knew he needed to let go of her hand, back up, cool down, but all his motor functions seemed to stop.

"We could use a blow dryer to dry your shirt."

"Oh. No." He forced his fingers to release her and take hold of the towel, careful not to touch her hand again. Taking a short step in retreat, he flashed a classic—and he hoped—nonchalant smile. "It will dry."

Shaking her head, she broke the connection, turned toward the sink, and reached for the hair dryer. "It would only take a second."

"I'm fine. It's drying already. Let's get back to work."

Slowly, reluctantly, she bobbed her head, blew out a resigned breath, and, stepping around him, returned to the outer room. Brad sucked in what little air was left in the small bathroom. Suddenly working side by side with Hope didn't seem like such a good idea anymore. *Note to self: do not stand close to Hope in confined spaces*. Especially since he was absolutely sure of one thing about this boss-incognito gig—shagging the head of housekeeping was most definitely not in his job description.

CHAPTER FOUR

*W*ow. The one word flashed in Hope's head like a neon sign. If her heart pounded any faster, it would break free of her chest and race out the building. All because of a man's simple hold of her wrist and the most intoxicating gray eyes she'd ever had the pleasure of falling into.

How long had it been since she'd felt anything even close to that kind of reaction from a man? Without turning, she felt Brad follow her from the bathroom. *Felt him.* Like the warm waves from a patio heater, she knew he'd walked past her to the other bed before glancing up to see him dumping the pillows from their cases. Maybe all these years without a man in her life was too long. Didn't what few friends she had tell her every chance they got that she was too young to be alone?

Brad shoved the used linens into the laundry bag and, standing at the foot of the bed, pulled the drawstring closed. "I'll take this to the chute."

All she could do was bob her head. Words were jumbled in confusion. Grappling with emotions she hadn't faced in so long, she had no idea what to do about any of it. Except make the beds and move on. She pulled clean sheets from her cart. That's how it worked. One step at a time. One task at a time. She was making way too much of a simple chemical reaction. None of this was any big deal. So the guy was too handsome for words. More than forty women would be arriving soon, and, for now, that was all that mattered.

"Want some help with that, or should I start with the next room?" Brad stood just inside the doorway.

No big deal. "Go ahead and do the other bed. Let's knock this out and call it in. If we can keep up the pace, we might pull this off."

Brad smiled, pushed away from the door, and her traitorous heart rate took off galloping again. This was going to be a long morning.

They'd made it through four more rooms, working in the same easy rhythm they'd established—before she'd discovered the man had dreamy eyes and a rock-solid chest that she had no business salivating over—when Sandy knocked on the door frame.

"Checkout is slowing down. Keith has it under control. Thought you could use an extra set of hands."

"Can I." Of all days for Lani to flake out on her, this had to be the worst. Even with a full staff, doing make-ready for a sold-out hotel was a stretch. This short-handedness was a nightmare.

"Where do I start?" Sandy literally rolled up her sleeves and, with a smile, rubbed her hands together. She *so* should have gotten the job as assistant manager. Not that Brad wasn't doing the position justice, but there had to be other hotels under the EastCo umbrella needing new management where he could have been sent. Maybe not on the Big island, but somewhere.

New management? Hope froze at the ugly thoughts flooding her mind. Was this guy really here to fill a gap or was he only the first of new management intended to replace the current guard? That's how EastCo worked and everyone knew it. The first replacement fills a void, then one by one the established loyal employees get booted for a company employee. Oh, Lord, she hoped not. Finding another job close to her home and Jason's school where she wouldn't have to work her way up all over again would not be easy. She'd looked for a lateral move to another hotel when the news of the buyout had first hit, but even with the booming tourism business and condominium complexes, opportunities were slim. No, her best option was to do everything in her power to keep the job she had.

Lost in thought, or nerves, she turned to find both Brad

and Sandy standing in front of her, waiting for their next instructions. Her cell phone sounded, and she hit Speaker. Nina needed more supplies.

Hope turned to Brad.

He was already moving out the door. "On my way."

"That leaves you and me to finish up the beds," Hope said to Sandy.

Without further instruction, Sandy moved to the opposite side of the room and stripped the bed. It took her a few quiet seconds before she cleared her throat and stuffed a pillow into a clean case. "How's he doing?"

"Not bad."

"Looks like a hard worker." She reached for another pillow.

"Better than I expected."

"I guess it was too much to hope he was a blithering idiot who tripped over his own feet."

Hope chuckled. "Could still happen."

A smile replaced Sandy's sullen expression. "I can hope." Snapping out the clean top sheet, she let it glide onto the bed. "Can I ask a question?"

"Of course." Hope already had her bed made and was walking over to help Sandy.

"You seem nervous. It's not like you to let a little time crunch ruffle your feathers. Is something wrong?"

"With me?" Hope tucked in the sheet corner. "No. Not at all."

Sandy tossed a pillow to Hope and reached for another. "You're sure?"

"Yeah. Just overworked, like the rest of us." Hope set the pillows across the headboard. It didn't strike her as a very good idea to mention how the new guy doing the job Sandy wanted had Hope overheated. Especially since she hadn't a clue what the heck she was going to do about it.

It was almost one o'clock, and, according to the clipboard

Hope kept checking off, they still had a few more rooms to go before the block reserved for the incoming group would be ready. For the last few rooms, Brad had been the one calling in the status reports. Picking up the phone to relay one more room was complete, the voice on the other end almost shouted, "Buses in the drive."

Red Hats arriving ten minutes early. They couldn't have been a dear and shown up ten minutes late? Or twenty? Hope set the last clean wastebasket in place when he hung up and gave her the news.

"The ladies are here."

"Okay." She sucked in a breath and blew it out. "What about the reward guests?"

"Room 322 just checked out." Brad repeated what Sandy had told him. "No word on 311."

"Good." She breathed deep again. "We'd better move it."

"Keith wants me at the front desk."

"Go." Hope was already in the hall, ready to move to the next room. "We can handle the last of this. I'll have Nina come for the supply cart. You do what they brought you here for." With a smile and a thumbs-up, she turned away, and shoved the empty cart up the hall.

Her last words made him feel like a heel. For the first time all day he felt like a lying fraud. A cheat. A spy. And there wasn't a blasted thing he could do about it. He'd committed to a two-week run for this gig, and he wasn't going to go back on his word over a guilty conscience. In fourteen days he'd move on, and no one would be the wiser that Brad Kane was one and the same with Bradford Peyton, CEO.

Taking the stairs instead of the elevator, he sprinted outside and took a shortcut across the central courtyard that connected some of the hotel's buildings to the lobby, ignoring the Do Not Walk On the Grass signs. It wasn't like anyone could actually fire him. In the lobby the bright colors worn by the new arrivals took him by surprise. Yes, he knew about Red Hat ladies. And, no, he'd never actually been in a room filled with women wearing red hats of every size and shape imaginable.

Across the lobby he caught Keith surveying the crowded space before addressing the customer in front of him. Next to him, holding out a room card, Sandy smiled at an older woman who appeared in no rush to give the next in line a chance to visit. Despite the request for early check-in, none of the laughing and chatting women scattered about the lobby appeared in any hurry.

With a handful of smiles and welcomes, Brad made his way to the Employees' Only door and hurried through the office to stand beside Keith. "What can I do?"

"Familiar with our system?" he asked in a whisper.

Brad had to shake his head. He'd never worked on any of the systems for any of the hotels he'd bought, sold, or kept through the years.

"Okay. Stay with me while I check in a few more people. When you think you can handle it on your own, take over this position, and I'll move to the computer at the end."

Brad nodded and watched in horror as seconds ticked by, waiting for fresh screens to appear after every step. "Is it always this slow?"

Keith nodded, swiped a credit card, and waited for the new screen. "Part of the terms for the sale was the Paradise Shores had to convert to Estacio's software."

"And that didn't help?"

The screen refreshed, and Keith entered the data and programmed the room key. "Help? Even if this new system had been better than what we had, which it isn't—"

"What do you mean, it isn't?" Brad had to lower his voice so the guests wouldn't overhear.

"It requires more steps than the software we used to have. Before, with the old system, available rooms were automatically integrated. Now we have to change from one screen to another to pull up and assign a room."

Brad didn't like the sound of that.

"Here you go, Ms. Holland. Elevators are across the lobby to your left. Enjoy your stay." Keith held out the room keys and pointed to the elevators with his other hand.

"I always do." The woman smiled back, turning and

handing the card to another woman beside her in a bright purple dress.

Keith tapped at the keyboard to call up the new screen as the next person in line approached. "Not only is this program not better than what we had, it didn't occur to anyone that we might need a hardware upgrade to use it."

"I see." Brad watched intently, taking in every step and kicking himself for what he'd thought had been a brilliant idea—one step closer to updating the hotel and putting it back on the market for a tidy profit. Nowhere in the reports he'd read did it mention inadequate hardware.

"How did it go making beds?" Keith asked quietly while waiting for the screen change.

"Fine. Could have bounced a quarter on them."

Keith looked at him sideways and held back a chuckle. "I wouldn't have pegged you for former military."

"I'm not."

"Thank you for your patience, Ms. Deleon." Keith held out the welcome card with the room key.

The larger-than-life woman flashed a huge grin that made her eyes sparkle. "It's not like I've got anywhere else to go."

Keith chuckled, gave the rest of his speech about amenities, elevators, and for her to let him know if she needed anything. Once again refreshing screens between guests. "We appreciate your help with the make-readies. I'll be sure it goes in my report to the new main office."

Brad almost laughed at that. "It's not like working with Hope was a hardship."

For a split second Keith's fingers froze over the keyboard, and Brad was reasonably certain it was not because of the software or hardware.

"Has she worked here long?"

This time Brad could see the tightening of Keith's jaw as he pressed down on his back teeth. "Yes, but I wouldn't get any ideas."

"Ideas?"

"She's a nice lady. She doesn't need to be tangled up in … anything." Keith attended to the next guest, his frustration with the new computer system and with Brad's comments about Hope well hidden.

Confident he could take on the incoming guests by himself, Brad opted to wait a while longer. He wanted to know more about Hope—and Keith—but chose not to speak until the current guest checking in had turned her back. "Then there's no husband?"

Keith shook his head.

"Boyfriend?"

Keith shot him a steely glare before turning his attention to the next guest.

Brad was a patient man; he could wait this out.

Another red-hat-wearing lady all checked in, Keith removed his fingers from the keyboard and turned to fully face Brad. "There is a strict policy of no fraternizing between upper management and employees. There are two upper management positions in this hotel. Mine and now apparently yours. Am I clear?"

"Crystal. I think I can handle this on my own now." As an afterthought, Brad pointed at the computer.

Keith took an extra long moment before nodding, then walked away.

Apparently Brad wasn't the only one to have Hope Gibbons get under his skin. The question at hand was, what was Brad going to do about it?

CHAPTER FIVE

"Four thirty. Not bad." Nina slid her card into the time clock.

"I can't wait until we're fully staffed again so I can get out the door on time." Under normal conditions, Hope could finish up and be out the door by four o'clock and get to Jason's school in time to avoid paying another hour of aftercare.

She still had another thirty minutes' worth of paperwork to do, but she was bone-tired and would probably do a better job after a good night's sleep. So Hope gathered her purse and flung it over her shoulder. Following Nina out the door, she pulled it shut behind them and turned the lock.

"I'm so pooped, my tired is tired." Nina held back a yawn.

"I know. It's the stress. Rushing is as mentally exhausting as physical efforts." Hope paused at the door to the ladies' room.

"Call me in the morning if Lani flakes again and you need me to come in."

"Thanks, but I'm sure she'll be here."

Nina walked away, shaking her head.

Hope couldn't blame her. Lani had become terribly unreliable, but, with three young children, Hope didn't have the heart to let her go.

Her reflection in the mirror showed what Hope already knew; she was working her butt off and not getting enough sleep. Even if she wanted a man, the way she looked now would scare even the most desperate away. Except Keith. She sucked in a breath and thought back to the tingles racing from her fingertips to her toes when Brad had grabbed her wrist. It hadn't been a gentle touch. He'd snatched her hard and hadn't let go, and her pulse had taken off like a greyhound after a rabbit.

Just remembering it had her heart racing once again. Why couldn't a nice guy like Keith send her senses reeling like that? Leaving her bag on the counter, she used the restroom, then washed her hands. Staring at her reflection again, she wondered when she had gotten so careless about her appearance. Her hair—twisted in a knot atop her head— had long ago tilted sideways, making her face look … unbalanced. With no makeup and dark circles under her eyes, she looked and felt a heck of a lot older than she was.

Removing the one pin in her hair and untying the bun, she ran her fingers along her scalp, shaking out the long strands. Somewhere in her purse she had one of those folding comb-brush combinations. Rummaging through tissues and crackers and gummy candy, she finally snagged what she'd been looking for. Carefully threading the comb through her tangles, she continued until her hair hung past her shoulders. She still looked exhausted, but at least she felt a little closer to human. Satisfied she wouldn't scare the crows, she gathered her belongings and hurried outside. If she didn't waste anymore time, she could make it to the elementary school before she ran into the next hour.

A small part of her felt a little ridiculous, taking time to fuss with her hair and daydreaming. Despite what her hormones were screaming, the last thing she needed in her life was the complication of a man. All she needed was the one man already in her life. Eight years old, with wavy blonde hair and big blue eyes.

Her bag in the passenger seat, Hope buckled in and turned the key. Nothing. Not a stutter. Not a groan. Silence. Painful silence. This made no sense. She'd just had the oil changed. The extra all-points-whatever check had said the car was good to go. Pumping the pedal the way she remembered seeing when she was a kid, she sucked in a wishful breath and, closing her eyes, turned the key again.

Nothing. A rapping on her window startled a gasp out her.

"Sorry. Need some help?" Brad stood, leaning down at her.

Fumbling at the door, she lowered the window. "The car won't start."

Brad leaned back and eyed her old car from front to rear and then leaned in again. "Turn the key."

She did as instructed. Still nothing.

"I'm not a mechanic, but my first guess is you need a new starter."

She didn't want to hear about anything that cost more than an oil change. Her budget was always stretched to the max and having to pay extra for afternoon daycare wasn't helping. "Maybe all I need is a jump?"

"I doubt it."

"How can you be so sure?"

One brow rose up, then relaxed. "You've got juice."

"How do you know?"

"This car isn't old enough to have manual windows, and you opened the window when I tapped on it."

"Oh." He was right. The key had been turned halfway between running and off. Just to be sure, she hit the map light, not at all happy when the singular beam shone down on her.

"If it were a bad battery, the engine would most likely have made some effort to turn over. But it's probably not the battery. Do you have someone you can call?"

Call. Murphy's law had struck again. In an effort to save money she'd canceled the roadside service she normally had. "No."

"A mechanic you use?"

She shook her head. The yogurt she'd inhaled at lunch soured in her stomach. "I have to pick up my son." Maybe she could pay for a car service. Not in the budget, but what choice did she have?

"Son?"

Hope snatched her purse off the passenger seat in search of her cell phone. "Jason. He goes to Kahuna Elementary, and I get charged more for aftercare if I go past the hour."

"I can give you a ride."

Her phone in hand, she balked at the unexpected offer. "You don't have to do that."

"No. I don't. But you need a ride. I have a car and no place immediate to be. Seems reasonable to me. Besides," his gaze softened, "I'd like to help."

The words, "Thank you," tumbled out before she had a chance to think this through all the way.

"Good. On the drive over we'll figure out what to do with your car."

Looking into those steel-gray eyes, Hope wished everything could be this simple. Car breaks down and Sir Lancelot with his white hatchback come to the rescue. But this was no fairy tale, and she had the craziest feeling that her broken-down car had just become the least of her problems.

Son? Hope looked way too young to have a son in school. Then again, most people thought Brad looked too young to be the CEO of a multibillion-dollar company. More than one.

And having a son wasn't the only surprise. When she exited the car and pulled to her full height, a cascade of thick blonde hair fell, caressing her shoulders. Good grief. Had he really thought her only a little bit pretty? Without a lick of makeup this woman was stunning. His mouth went instantly dry. What wouldn't he give to change places with those golden locks and run his hand down her neck, across her shoulders and back up to the moist lips she was nibbling on.

Keeping his mouth shut, not that he could find something reasonable to say even if he wanted to, he waved her forward and took an extra second to breathe deep and get his head on straight. At his car, their hands momentarily collided as they both reached for the passenger door handle at the same time. The electricity zapped though him even stronger than it had earlier in the hotel. "Allow me."

"Oh," she mumbled and stepped back, then, eyes down, slid into the seat.

Buckled in and engine rumbling, he put the car in gear and focused on the way out, not on the woman at his side. A task easier said than done. "Which way?"

"Left." She studied him as he exited the lot and turned as directed.

"Now what?"

"You're not from around here?"

He shook his head.

"When you come to the traffic light, turn right. You'll see the school down the road a piece on the left."

"Got it."

"So how long have you lived in the area?"

"I haven't. I just got here." He turned at her silence and was greeted by those beautiful green eyes, big and round with surprise.

"So they moved you here for this job?"

"Sort of."

Her eyes grew even wider, filling with questions.

"This assignment may not be permanent," he felt obligated to mention.

"May not?"

"The Paradise Shores is understaffed, and I was the closest to come help."

"Oh." Her voice took on a happier tone that spread to her eyes. What was that all about?

"That anxious to get rid of me?" The idea bothered him more than it should have.

"Oh, no. Not at all. It's just that ..." her cheeks flushed a pretty shade of pink.

He liked it. He seemed to like every new thing he learned about this woman. Maybe a little bit too much.

He waited an extra beat or two for her to finish. "Just what?"

"Well," she folded her hands in her lap, her thumbs wrestling each other. "Sandy has been filling in as assistant manager, and we all ... we'd hoped she'd get the job permanently."

That would explain the momentary chill Brad had seen in Sandy's gaze when they'd been introduced. "She seems to be good at her job."

"Very good. Way better than the idiot before her." Hope pointed to the left with her hand. "There it is. The school."

Brad turned into the long semicircular drive in the front of the rectangular building. "I'll wait here."

"Thanks. Be right back."

As soon as the door of the building had slammed shut behind her, he tapped his phone.

"Hey, man," John answered. "Is it a yes for dinner?"

"I don't think so. Do you have a mechanic you can recommend?"

"Yeah."

"Good. Text me his info. One of the women working at the hotel has a dead car in the parking lot, and she doesn't have a trustworthy mechanic of her own."

"Will do."

"Oh—and, John?"

"Yeah?"

"Give the mechanic a heads-up. Tell him to charge some ridiculously low price. I'll cover the difference. I don't think she's got much money."

Silence hung briefly between them. "You certain you want to do that?"

"Yeah. Tell him to check out the car for anything else that might be ready to go and handle that too."

"Sure you don't want to just buy her a new car?" his friend teased.

"Don't be a jerk."

"Hey, women like that sort of thing."

Maybe some women. The kind both he and John had too often dangled as arm candy. "Not this kind."

John remained quiet, and Brad didn't like the idea of

what his friend was thinking. Probably because it was most likely the same thing he was thinking. *What was so special about this woman?*

CHAPTER SIX

ow did this happen? One minute Hope was leaving
work to pick up her son from school, like any other
day of the week. Her only plans for the evening to
stop at the grocery mart, and later soaking in her bathtub
before bed.

Instead she, Jason and Brad were sharing a pizza at her
son's favorite dinner spot. And even more surprising, Brad
Kane, the man she'd originally pegged as all looks and no
substance, had spent most of the time they'd been here
oohing and aching over her son's schoolwork.

"You can have this one if you want." The little boy
shoved a sheet of paper from art class overrun with colored
squiggles and a gold star affixed to the upper corner.

Even Hope had no idea what the drawing was supposed
to be. Did she even have art class at his age?

"It's beautiful. I know just where to hang it." Brad held
the proffered drawing as though it were a valuable Picasso.

Across the table, sitting at Hope's side, Jason pushed a
sheet with multiplication problems along with another gold
star. His teacher was big on stickers to encourage the
children to work hard. "You can have this too."

"Very good." Brad curled his fingers under and
extended his hand to Jason for the newly learned fist bump.
So far, every time Brad found a reason to congratulate her
son with the bumping-of-knuckles gesture, Jason giggled
and laughed as though it were the coolest thing since
chocolate chip cookies.

With her son having such a good time, Hope found it
easy to sit back and enjoy the pleasantness—and not think
about her car, the starter, or how she would afford this new

hiccup in her life.

"Jason!" Bradley, a boy in her son's class, came barreling across the restaurant, waving a white ball in the air. "Look what I got."

Crossing the room on the little boy's heels, his parents waved at Hope, coming to a halt by the table. "If we'd known you and Jason would be here, we would have skipped the sporting goods store."

"It was a spur-of-the-moment thing," Hope responded. The parents, whose names she couldn't remember, cast a quick glance from Hope to the two boys in a near frenzy over the new baseball, only to land and remain on Brad. Hope gestured toward him. "This is a new coworker."

"Nick Harper." The father introduced himself, staring at the man as though he had a speck of spinach between his teeth, then gestured to his wife.

Looking less quizzical than her husband and juggling a cute little girl with her daddy's big blue eyes on her hip, the woman smiled at Brad and extended her hand. "Kara."

On his feet now, Brad shook her hand. "Brad Kane. Nice to meet you."

"Same here," the man mumbled, shaking his head and turning his attention back to Hope. "The sign-ups for baseball opened today. You'll have to hurry if we want the boys on the same team."

"Yes, well …" Hope sucked in her lips, debating how to politely back out without coming right out and saying she couldn't afford the registration fee or the accessories Jason would need. Last year it had been much easier to slide by without signing Jason up, but this year his growing friendship with the Harper boy made staying on the sidelines more of a challenge.

"Can I have a baseball too?" Her son tugging at her right arm and waving the white ball in her face interrupted her search for words. "Can I?"

"I … uh … We'll see."

This time Brad's brows knit together at her awkward response.

"It's getting late," she continued. "We don't want to

abuse Mr. Kane's hospitality." Hope looked up at Nick Harper and his wife, not wanting them to misunderstand the situation. "My car wouldn't start after work. Brad was kind enough to play chauffeur for the evening."

Deep blue eyes narrowed and Nick Harper turned a concerned gaze her way. "I've been known to tinker a bit here or there. Maybe I can be of help?"

Kara slipped her hand into the curve of her husband's elbow. "If you need a bomb disarmed, he'd be your man."

"Uh," Hope wasn't sure what to say about that.

Kara chuckled. "Nick's former Navy EOD."

Even hope knew EOD stood for explosive ordinance disposal.

"Any good at starters?" Brad's words came out pleasant enough, but the look he shot Nick didn't seem quite as receptive.

Nick's gaze didn't seem any more sure of the man he was sizing up than Brad's had. "You know cars?"

"Enough to know that if her lights and radio work, it's not the battery or the alternator."

Lips pressed tightly, Nick bobbed his head and raked his fingers through thick dark curls. "Replacing starters is one level above my paygrade."

"What about Doug?" his wife brightened. "That man can fix anything at the shop."

Nick hefted one shoulder, keeping his eyes on Brad. "Maybe, but even we send the boats to a real mechanic for engine work." He seemed to study Brad rather intently and she wasn't sure what was running through Nick's head, but she had the feeling more than her car's future relied on his conclusions.

"I actually have the name of a highly recommended mechanic," Brad offered.

This time Nick glanced at Hope.

"An affordable one," Brad added.

Nick's gaze darted back to Brad and then she saw it. The decision had been made. Nick Harper leaned into his wife and shifted their daughter onto his shoulders. "Sounds like you've got it covered. Let us know if you need anything."

"We'd better go order that pizza." His wife announced to their son.

"Can't I play a little while with Jason?" The boy nearly whined.

"It looks like they're ready to go." Kara brushed the boy's curly hair.

The disappointment in both boys tugged at Hope. "I suppose a few minutes will be fine."

"Yay." The two boys jumped up and down, Jason waving his friend's brand-new baseball in the air at the same time Hope opened her purse and dug out her wallet. Fortunately the boys' two favorite games were some of the least expensive options in the arcade section of the pizza parlor.

"I've got this." Nick Harper handed his son a ten-dollar bill.

Much more than what she'd intended to give Jason.

While Jason's friend took the money and bolted for the arcade section, Jason paused long enough to thank his benefactor before running after the boy with the cash.

"He's a good boy," Kara Harper smiled. "I'm glad they're friends."

Hope couldn't say anything over the lump lodged in her throat. A simple acknowledgment of Jason had her proud enough to puff out her chest and strut around the room.

Brad sat and leaned forward over the table holding out his phone. "Here's the name and number my friend who lives in the area gave me the name for an excellent and affordable mechanic."

"Oh, well I suppose I can give him a call, but I'm sure Nina knows—"

"He's waiting for your call."

For a few seconds Hope wasn't sure if she should be relieved or annoyed at the help. She'd been taking care of herself and Jason for a long time now and didn't need anyone butting in unasked. Another side of her was awfully glad not to have to do it all alone for once. And the awfully glad side won out over her stubborn—and probably misplaced—pride.

"Okay," Kara leaned into her husband. "What has your feathers in a dither?"

"I don't know." He cast a quick glance over his shoulder at Jason's mom and her new friend.

Kara followed his gaze. "He seems nice enough."

"Yeah. For just a minute I got a vibe that said something wasn't right."

"But…?"

"It didn't last."

"Well that's good. I like her. Not that I know her that well, but she works hard, too hard I think."

"It can't be easy raising a boy alone."

Kara knew Nick's mind was going to Patty Ann and the years she'd had to raise Bradley on her own. "If it makes you feel any better my creep alarm hasn't gone off.

"It does," he smiled down at her.

"But, if you want, I can think up an excuse to call her tomorrow, maybe a play date or something, make sure everything is all right."

"Yeah," Nick nodded. "I would."

Brad waited impatiently as Hope spoke with the mechanic John had recommended. Every few seconds he shifted his attention to the two boys, delighted with some game across the way. All he could see were the boys slamming a massive rubber bat randomly across a table in front of them.

Listening to Hope and watching Jason, Brad was torn between staying at the table to make sure everything worked out as he'd planned and checking on the boys to ensure all was well. Though he wasn't sure why he was worried about Jason; ten dollars seemed like more than enough to keep them busy, and, even at thirty-five years old, Brad would have been thrilled to spend many an afternoon whacking away life's irritations. The two kids were probably happier without his interference. Not to mention his friend's dad was keeping an eagle eye on them from the take out counter.

"I see. ... Thank you. Yes. I'll meet you in one hour." Hope swiped at the phone and handed it back to him. "You're right. Fingers crossed he's as good a mechanic as he seems to be a nice man."

"Oh?"

"Since he has his own tow truck, he's offered to bring my car to his shop at no charge. He'll take a look at it first thing in the morning, and, if I'm not happy with his estimate, he'll take the car anywhere I want."

Relieved, Brad leaned back in his chair. He had no idea why, but, for some reason, it mattered a great deal to him that Hope didn't have to spend the night worrying about her car. That left him wondering what the deal was with baseball. From the look on her face when the other boy's parents spoke of baseball, he got the impression she didn't like the idea of having him play and had no intention of letting Jason join the team. "So the problem with the car is solved."

She hesitated and nibbled on her lower lip the way she'd done earlier.

He made a valiant effort not to volunteer to nibble on that luscious lip for her.

"Could I trouble you to give us a lift back to the hotel instead of my place?"

"Of course. You said it yourself. I'm your chauffeur for the night."

With the exceptions of the bright smiles she'd bestowed on her son as he'd shared his schoolwork with them, this was the first time since leaving work that she'd really smiled at Brad, and he liked it. Very much.

"That will be a huge help."

"My pleasure." Brad cast a glance in the boys' direction. Still whacking away with massive foam bats. "The Harpers are right. He's a nice boy."

"Thank you." She beamed again. "Do you have children?"

He shook his head.

"Nieces? Nephews?"

His head turned from side to side again. "'Fraid not. Only child. You?"

"Just me. And Jason."

Brad wasn't sure how welcome his next question would be. "What about Jason's father? Where is he?"

The solemn curtain that drew down over her eyes surprised him. He'd expected an angry ex story but not sorrow.

"He's gone."

It took Brad a few seconds to process her choice of words and tone, and suddenly his heart ached for her. "How long?"

"Over eight years."

Doing fast math in his head, Brad figured Jason couldn't be much older than that. "Then Jason was only—"

"Not even born yet." She shifted her gaze to her son, and Brad could see her spine straighten and her chin rise, drawing from a well of strength somewhere deep inside. "His father never knew about him."

"Grandparents?"

She shook her head. "No one."

God. He might be an only child, but he still had an extended family of cousins and aunts and uncles and grandparents. Though, at this stage of his life, he could probably handle what fate threw his way on his own, but that didn't mean he wanted to. "I'm sorry."

"I don't know why I'm telling you all this. I barely know you."

"Because I asked?"

That had her chuckling.

He much preferred the happy Hope.

"I'd better get my son. I still have a lot to work through, and we have a strict rule about bedtime."

Brad rose and circled the small table to reach for the back of her chair. "All rules were meant to be broken once in a while."

"Thank you." Hope pushed to her feet. "Not bedtime.

Growing children need their sleep."

Brad nodded. He was pretty sure he'd read that somewhere, and, even if he hadn't, it made perfect sense. "So what else do you have to work out?"

"Nothing for you to lose sleep over." Hope crossed the play area, Brad following her to Jason's side. "Time to go, sweetie."

"Just a little longer?" Jason swung the massive bat at what Brad could see was a newer version of Whack-A-Mole.

"Sorry. Tonight we have to meet the man who'll fix Mommy's car tomorrow."

Tomorrow. Of course. He should have thought this car thing through all the way. "Listen." Brad moved closer. "About tomorrow. What time do you need me to pick you up?"

Hope whirled around. "That won't be necessary."

"Do I need to give you my entire no-I-don't-have-to-but-I-want-to lecture again?"

"No." Her lips curled at the corners. "Thank you."

He loved it when she smiled.

"I usually drop Jason off at school at eight o'clock and punch in at the hotel by 8:30. Will 7:45 be good?"

"Perfect."

"Okay boys, one last game." She eased back watching the sheer glee on the boys' faces.

He understood exactly what she must be thinking about. Nothing to worry about in life except getting gold stars on papers and smacking a mole with a rubber bat.

"Yay." The boys cheered when the game was over. "We won."

Brad had no idea who the *we* was, but they spun around grinning like cartoon cats.

"Let's walk Bradley back to his parents." Hope put a protective hand over each boys' shoulder. Loose enough to nudge, tight enough to keep them from bolting across the crowded restaurant. He liked that. The world could use a few more mothers like her raising the next generation.

"Thank Mr. Harper," Hope encouraged.

"Thank you." Jason beamed.

"Anytime," Nick Harper replied, pizza carton in hand, and turned to Hope. "Same goes for your mom. If you need anything at all, we're big on being neighborly."

Kara rolled her eyes, "Not that island folk aren't friendly but we're both originally from Texas. You know, everything is bigger there. Including nosy but helpful neighbors."

Hope laughed, not smiled, not grinned, laughed. A beautiful sound that hit Brad hard in the gut. "Thank you again."

During the short ride to the hotel, Jason talked nonstop about his friend and baseball, and, with every mention of anything related to the sport, Hope tensed in her seat. Something wasn't right. What could she possibly have against baseball? What else was he missing?

"Are you seriously that daft?" Ava Maplewood leaned forward in her seat.

Apparently Brad was, and his hostess was about to give him a clue. After taking Hope to the hotel to hand over her keys to the mechanic, making sure the guy was as good as John suggested, and then dropping her and her son off safely in their apartment, his phone had rung.

Since Ava was eager to hear how his first day of work had gone, she and John had hurried home from dinner at her mother's and invited Brad over for coffee or a night cap.

It hadn't taken long to share the issues and concerns from the hotel—though it had taken Ava a while to stop laughing at bedmaking 101—when he'd moved on to Hope, her car, and the baseball thing. Whatever he'd said had lit a fire under his best friend's wife.

"You'd better lay it on him," John suggested to his wife at Brad's silence.

"First, you two men will get an earful from Hope if she ever finds out how you're working behind her back. I cannot even begin to fathom what her reaction will be when she discovers that Brad Kane is really Bradford Peyton."

Brad opened his mouth to protest, but Ava held out her hand to silence him.

"I know you're supposed to be undercover but that's work. Fixing cars and pizza dinners is an entire different thing and you don't lie to a woman about who you are or how you're helping her."

"I—"

Ava's hand remained palm out in his face. "Second, I know it seems small to you, but, from what little you've said, she clearly is a woman who works hard to provide well for her son, and she won't take kindly to what she perceives as charity."

"It's not charity," the two men echoed.

"I'd help you two if you needed me," Brad added.

"Whatever." Ava sighed, slapping her arms at her sides. "But if you figured out car repairs would strain her budget, how can you not get that she probably doesn't have a budget for Little League?"

"Budget for baseball?" Now Brad was really confused. "What's to budget? Twelve kids, one bat, a few balls."

Ava rolled her eyes, and Brad could see the steam building. "I keep forgetting how clueless you guys can be to the real world. Okay." She inched farther onto the edge of her seat. "First, there has to be a registration fee. It could be fifteen dollars or fifty. I don't know, but I guarantee, whatever it is, it's not in a single-mom's budget. Then there's the equipment her son needs. She'll have to buy him shoes—"

"It's Little League. He won't need cleats," John dared to add despite his wife's glare.

"All the little boys will have new shoes for baseball. They won't be playing in the shoes they wear to school. She'll have to buy Jason a pair as well. And a uniform. More money she probably doesn't have. And then a glove."

Brad was doing the math in his head. No matter how he ran the numbers for an eight-year-old, Brad wasn't coming in at much more than one or two hundred dollars.

"Being on a team comes with team activities. Practice. Who's going to get him to and from practice? Is it while she works?"

Brad shrugged.

Ava shot him a see-what-I-mean look and continued talking. "Teams who play together tend to eat together. After practice maybe but after games definitely. So now she has to add eating out once or twice a week to her budget. And she'll have no control over where they go, but my guess is somewhere with entertainment for the boys, which means more money to spend so he can participate."

The ten-dollar bill Nick Harper had forked over for a few minutes of playtime came to mind. Nothing to Brad, but he was starting to understand that, every time Hope nibbled on that lower lip of hers, she was adding up the dollar signs in her head. Ava was right. He was daft. But the real question was, now that he understood, what was he going to do about it?

CHAPTER SEVEN

Hunched over her desk at work, Hope disconnected the call and stared at her phone. "I don't get it."

"What don't you get?" Nina asked.

"This mechanic. I thought maybe he was just being nice, not charging for the towing, because he knew he'd make up for it with the work today."

"Sound reasonable," Nina agreed.

"He says he has a used starter that came with some parts another client paid for but didn't use. All he's asking is $100 for labor. He'll deliver the car for me this afternoon if I want him to do the work."

"A hundred dollars? What's the guy's name and number?"

"Yeah. Like I said, I don't get it."

"Who cares! Tell him to fix the car and light a candle at church on Sunday to thank the Lord."

"I did. Tell him to fix it, that is."

"So why do you look so unsettled?"

"I don't know. I guess you're right. I shouldn't look a gift horse in the mouth." The office phone rang, startling Hope out of her thoughts. "Housekeeping."

"Keith wants all department heads in the lunchroom now," Sandy informed her. "He says not to freak. It's not bad news."

"Thanks. I'm on my way."

"Now what?" Nina asked.

"Don't know. Managers meeting for 'not bad' news."

Nina laughed. "That's a first. Maybe you should buy a lottery ticket today."

"Right. Hold down the fort for me. Hopefully this won't take long."

Hurrying along, lost in a myriad of possibilities for the impromptu meeting, she wasn't paying attention and turned the corner at the end of the hall and slammed full speed ahead into a human wall. One with strong hands that grabbed her arms to steady her and sent instant heat waves rushing to her extremities and other inappropriate body parts. *Brad.*

"Sorry. You okay?" he asked softly.

"Yeah, I wasn't looking where I was going."

His fingers lingered another second on her arms, and, nodding, he released his hold but didn't move. "I was coming to see if you'd heard anything about your car."

Her car. Why couldn't she think straight with those amazing gray eyes staring at her? Why did this man so easily scramble all her senses? *Her car.* "Yes."

Brad didn't shift his gaze, didn't move, and, for a split second, Hope wondered if bumping into her had rattled him as much as it had her. He blinked, the tip of his tongue peeked out to moisten his lips, but, rather than glide across, it quickly slid back into his mouth.

The brief motion captured all her attention and raised the voltage on the waves still coursing through her system.

Blinking again, he took a small step in retreat, yet his eyes remained pinned to hers. "What did he say?"

"Say?" Right, the car. The mechanic. Hope stepped back as well. "He'll fix it and bring the car to me before the end of day."

"Excellent. Glad it worked out." His head bobbed, but his gaze remained fixed on her. "I guess I should get back to work. Keith has me shadowing Geraldo from maintenance."

"Oh." Sandy's call shoved its way to the forefront of Hope's scrambled thoughts. "There's a managers meeting in the lunchroom. That's where I was heading."

"Oh?" The stormy look in his eyes took on an intrigued sparkle.

"Yeah. Since you're management, you might as well make a U-turn."

"Yes, ma'am." He did that mock-salute thing he'd done the day before, but this time the only emotions stirring had nothing to do with tears.

Brad was going to have to give his assistant at headquarters a bonus for moving so fast. Most of last night, after leaving the Maplewood home, Brad had considered Ava's words carefully. Finally, somewhere around three o'clock this morning, it occurred to him the only way to make an unnoticed difference for Hope would be to do it for everyone.

"I received an executive memo from EastCo's main office about fifteen minutes ago." Keith held up a stack of papers. "I went ahead and printed a copy for each of you." He passed the stack around.

All eyes in the room were riveted on Keith. Most of them frowning, but a few widened like a spooked owl as the notice reached them.

Keith smiled and read from his copy. "In an attempt to compensate staff loyalty for remaining with the Paradise Shores Hotel and assuming the additional workload during the transfer of ownership, EastCo is gifting each and every Paradise Shores employee with one thousand dollars to be dispersed immediately."

An eruption of applause, mingled with hoots and cheers, interrupted Keith's speech. The energy level in the room had ramped up considerably, and Brad found himself caught up in the clapping and hooting. For him one thousand dollars was pocket money, but seeing the relief and joy in each person's eyes as they spoke to one another about what they would do this windfall had him riding on a cloud. As more of the employees' words registered with him, the elation he felt started to ebb. Expecting to hear about new clothes, a vacation, or some fanciful toy, words like *repairs, prescriptions, bank letters*, and *collection calls* stunned him silent.

He turned his attention to Hope; the smile on her face was exactly what he'd wanted to see. But was the money he'd meant to funnel through for Jason's summer ball needed for more critical bills?

Hope spun around and flashed a huge smile at him. "Better than playing the lottery."

"Excuse me?" he asked.

"Nina said today was a special day, and I should play the lottery. This is just as good." Her smile slipped. "You don't look very pleased. Is something wrong?"

"Oh," He forced his charming smile. "No. Just thinking about a few bills."

"Yeah." She sighed, but her smile remained in place, easing his concerns. "This will be a nice boost for a lot of people. I'd better run. I need to tell my staff." With a light pat on his arm. she popped up from her seat and hurried away.

The loud hum of voices eased as each manager left the room to spread the good news.

Ava was right. Bradford Peyton had a lot to learn.

A chorus of "Oh, my God" echoed in the tiny housekeeping office. Rather than traipsing through the entire complex to tell her staff one by one about the corporate gift, or make them wait until the end of day, Hope had merely summoned them all to her office. Once she'd given the initial information, she hadn't gotten in another word.

The news couldn't have been better timed. She'd pay off the credit card she'd used for the car repair, enroll Jason in baseball, and have a little bit left over to put away for the next unplanned expense. Nina was right. Hope just might pick up a lottery ticket today.

The giggles and laughter came to a screeching halt, and then the women—crammed in the room like sardines in a can—one by one scurried from the office and back to work. When the last person turned the corner, Hope realized who had been the catalyst for this unexpected dedication to their jobs.

Arms crossed, Brad stood grinning at the doorway. "I gather the news went over well."

"Like water at Niagara."

"I thought we could celebrate."

"Celebrate?"

"Yes. Together. Tonight."

A date? The man was asking her on a date? At least she thought it was a date. Actually she wasn't even all that sure she'd been asked. "I have Jason."

Letting his arms drop to his side, Brad pushed away from the door frame and sauntered over to her desk. He didn't walk. Didn't meander. The man practically oozed across the tiny office. "I didn't mean to exclude him. I have it on good authority that Chuck E. Cheese's is *the* place to celebrate with an eight-year-old."

She didn't have the heart to tell him Jason had outgrown the oversized mouse years ago, not that it mattered. Dating was not a good idea. "I don't know."

"I can pick you up around five thirty. Give you time to do homework or any other afterschool chores." His confidant stance slipped. "Do eight-year-olds have homework?"

A soft rumble of laughter escaped her lips before she could stop herself. She didn't know what to make of the suave man whose good looks had fooled her into thinking he was a man of little substance, but she was really starting to like the normal guy underneath. "I suppose an evening of fun and games, and pizza again, is in order."

"Wonderful. See you at five thirty." He hesitated just long enough that Hope thought he had something else to say, but then he smiled brightly and turned away.

How about that? She had a date. A date. She almost felt like giggling. The end of day couldn't come fast enough.

"You look awfully happy." Keith came into her small office and leaned against her desk. "You're smiling like the company gave you a lot more than a thousand dollars."

Had she been smiling that big? Her mind had been stuck on her date. "It's been a good day."

"How about we make it an even better day. What do

you say? You and me. We'll celebrate in style."

Now that was an obvious invitation. One she hated to turn down. "I'm sorry, but Jason and I already have plans."

His smile remained in place, but the twinkle in his eye disappeared.

She hated that she'd done that.

"Another time maybe."

"Keith …"

"I know." This time the smile vanished. "Can't blame a guy for trying."

"No. I guess I can't." Though she didn't feel it anymore, she tried to smile and felt a teeny bit better when he smiled back before walking away.

Eight years and not a single man worth the trouble, and now she had two. Life had a crazy sense of humor.

CHAPTER EIGHT

"It's so easy to make friends at that age." Hope watched her son and two other boys climbing like monkeys through the tube system wrapping around the large room.

"He probably gets it from his mom." Brad had moved from across the table to sit next her.

"I doubt that. Making friends wasn't easy for me growing up." Shuffled around from foster home to foster home, she'd learned a lot of life's lessons, but making friends and keeping them hadn't been one. It was one of the many things she and Dave had had in common. Like her, he'd lived in a foster home. Though almost fourteen when he'd lost his parents, he hadn't been in the system nearly as long as she had. At eighteen he'd enlisted, and at twenty-five he'd been home on rotation and, choosing the same movie she had, sat down the row from her. After the show he'd invited her for a drink. They wound up at the diner, eating pie. She'd fallen for him hard and fast. "I think he gets it from his dad."

"You think?"

"We weren't together very long."

"What happened to him?"

"Overseas. One of those suicide bombers. Or maybe it was a bomb in the road. I don't really remember. One of his buddies knew about me. He sent me a note on Dave's computer."

"Didn't the military contact you?"

She reached for the ring that was no longer on her finger. "We weren't married. They'd moved up his deployment unexpectedly. He knew I'd always dreamed of a big wedding so we decided to wait till he came home. He was only supposed to be gone a year."

"You didn't know you were pregnant?" Brad's voice came across so low he almost whispered.

She shook her head and looked at her son crawling noses to heels with his new friends.

Brad lifted his gaze to follow hers.

Sometimes if Jason looked at her just right, he reminded her a little of his dad. "Enough about me. Tell me about Brad Kane, only child. What else?"

"Not much to tell. I grew up on the East Coast, New England Brat, College in Boston," he didn't think mentioning Harvard right now was a good idea, "Graduated with a degree in international business. Still single. No children. Though my parents probably pray nightly to the patron saint of fertility for that to change."

Hope chuckled. "Is there such a thing?"

"Honestly? I think there are several. Though they're probably not called that exactly."

"How did you wind up in the hotel business?" His response was so slow in coming, she almost thought he wasn't going to answer.

"Opportunity and timing," he finally said.

"How are you liking Paradise Shores?"

One side of his mouth tilted up in a wry grin. "More than I expected."

"Really?" She didn't know what to make of this guy. Sometimes he seemed like an ordinary but exceptionally nice guy, and sometimes she got the feeling she was playing with fire.

"Listen. Yesterday at the pizza place the other boy's dad mentioned baseball. Is Jason going to play?"

Tonight she could answer without hesitation. "I signed him up online this afternoon."

"Good." Brad's grin stretched across his face, the happy-guy grin that made her stomach do little flips. "Then you haven't picked out any of his gear yet?"

"No." The league sent a list along with the confirmation of registration. It seemed simple enough. "Maybe we'll go on Saturday."

"Have someone to help pick out what you want?"

"I wouldn't think I'd need help for one little boy. Would I?"

Brad chuckled, and her insides flipped over the other way. "No. I wouldn't think so, but I'd love to tag along. It's been a while since I was in Little League, but I think it would be fun."

"You're volunteering to go shopping with me and my son?"

"Yes."

"Is this another one of those impending no-you-don't-have-to lectures?"

He laughed even harder. "It is."

"Then I guess, if you have nothing better to do on Saturday, you're welcome to join us."

"It's a date." Without waiting for her response, he turned his head toward the boys.

She was really getting to like this dating thing. She just hoped he didn't turn out to be a serial killer in disguise or a lying scumbag with a wife and two point five children back in New England.

Somewhere inside every grown man was a small part of him that would always be a little boy. The little boy in Brad wished they could have gone shopping for Jason's baseball supplies tonight. Hope had casually mentioned that after this evening's adventures Jason would be out like a light the second his head hit the pillow. She was only off by a few minutes.

From the rearview mirror Brad could see the little boy was already soundly asleep in the backseat.

Only one more block until he'd pull into the large lot for Hope's apartment complex. The section of town she lived in bordered a rather expensive area and belonged to an excellent school. Living in the humble, but well-kept neighborhood no doubt came with the perks of more affordable rents and the benefits of the better nearby elementary school.

Turning into the lot and taking the space closest to her door, Brad slipped the car into Park and turned off the engine. "Looks like he didn't quite make it to his pillow."

"Give me a few minutes to unlock the door, and I'll come back and get him." Hope unbuckled her seat belt.

"I'll help."

"You don't …" She bit her lower lip, the words she was about to add dying on her lips, and chuckled. "Thank you."

They were making progress. Next time he wanted to do something for her, hopefully she wouldn't protest at all. "My pleasure."

Brad opened the car door, unbuckled Jason's seat belt, practically dragged him from the car before tossing the boy over his shoulder, and, despite the juggling to get Jason into a comfortable carrying position, the squirt never blinked. Kids really did sleep like logs.

Up the stairway, Hope held open her front door. "Follow the hall to the bedroom."

Behind him, her low heels clicked against the tile floor. "His bed is on the left," she whispered.

The average-size bedroom had a twin bed on either side. Brad laid down Jason and Hope immediately stripped him of his shoes and socks.

"Anything else I can do?"

She nodded. "His pajamas are on a hook at the back of the bedroom door."

Retracing his steps, Brad closed the door and found two hooks. One higher up that held what had to be Hope's nightgown. Most of the women he'd known in recent years slept in some comfortable combination of shorts and a cami top or a skimpy negligee. He couldn't remember the last time he'd seen a woman in a full-length nightgown. On a lower hook, level with the doorknob, was a pair of Ninja Turtle pajamas. *Bingo.*

Standing next to the bed, he handed Hope the pajamas. "When he's out, he's really out."

"Just like a rag doll."

In no time, Hope had the boy in his nightwear and tucked under the blankets. Only a few minutes after that, she and Brad stood in the middle of the living room.

"Could I interest you in a cup of coffee or tea?" she asked.

"Coffee would be nice." He followed her the few feet into the tiny kitchen. Leaning back against the counter, he could take in pretty much the entire apartment. From what he could see, the place only had one bedroom. "Do you share the bedroom with Jason?"

"Sometimes." She lifted her chin, pointing toward the living room. "The sofa opens. I usually sleep there."

"When do you sleep in the other room?"

"Once in a while he'll have a bad dream, or we'll do an indoor campout. On the odd day that I have to put in extra hours or fill in for a sick housekeeper—"

"Like yesterday?"

"Exactly like yesterday. Nothing replaces a real bed." She pulled two cups from the upper cupboards. "How do you take your coffee?"

"Black."

"Well, that's easy." With her back to him, she continued to move about the small space, pulling out spoons and saucers while the older coffeemaker spewed steam.

"How long have you lived here?"

"Since Jason started school. I had to choose between a better school and backyard."

"And you picked the school."

"We can always go play in a park. But these are the important years to establish his education base." The machine stopped making noises, and she filled two cups. "I keep saying someday I'll go back to school, get a degree, make more money. But then I come home dead tired and think living in an apartment isn't so horrible. I mean, lots of people buy condos. It's pretty much the same thing."

"I suppose." He refrained from launching into the tax and real estate benefits of owning property. Especially since, at this moment, alarm bells sounded in the back of his head. All management positions with EastCo companies, including hotel housekeeping managers, required a college degree.

"Did I lose you?" Hope stood, holding out a cup of coffee to him.

"No. Sorry. My mind wandered."

"Hard day?" She turned and strolled into the living room, taking a spot on the edge of the sofa, immediately kicking off her shoes and tucking her feet underneath her.

"Not really hard, just busy." The only skin showing was her knees and yet, he couldn't seem to stop staring at them. What was wrong with him? Even leg men didn't get all bent out of shape over four inches of exposed knee.

She blew on the hot coffee. "Geraldo is a nice guy. His eldest son just came to work with us." Once again she puckered her lips creating ripples along the top of the warm liquid, and had successfully captured his attention away from her knees.

"So he said." Brad dragged his attention away from her pursed lips, still blowing on the steaming liquid, to something safer, like the dark brew in his own cup. "He's got a good handle on the property. I was rather surprised by all the repairs he could do without calling in outside help."

"Experience counts for a lot." She slurped a tiny sip.

"More than a lot." He forced himself to keep his gaze on his own mug. "There was a sewer line break. He determined it was halfway between the Gardenia building and the parking lot. Had the grounds crew digging up the lines."

"Mmm. I noticed the activity."

He chanced looking up and meeting her gaze. "Any other maintenance crew I've worked with would have had a plumbing company handle the whole thing. This extra effort probably saved the parent company quite a bit of money."

"Yeah, well be thankful you weren't shadowing the ground crew today or you would have been shoveling back there with them."

The sweetness of her smile gave him an unexpected jolt. It took him a few seconds for his thoughts and mouth to connect. "Keith explained that, until he gets notified otherwise, he's following the former owner's manager trainee program. Hands-on in every department before a full-time manager rotation." The best way to keep the conversation on business was to focus on his coffee and the day. The system for training in place fell in line with what Brad's plans had been, but, after only a day working on broken thermostats, dead sockets, and stopped-up toilets, he was beginning to appreciate the old guard's methods of retaining loyal staff rather than bringing in the supposedly brightest and best.

"You'll be assigned the night shift first." Tilting her chin up and swallowing the last drop, she exposed the silken smoothness of a long neck and Brad reminded himself to keep his eyes anywhere but on her.

"That's fine. I tend to be a night owl." He also had to remind himself that he didn't plan on being here long enough to be worked into the schedule, and that he certainly did want to rethink his original plans for the Paradise Shores' future. "Do you like your job?"

"I do." She set down her cup and shifted, letting her feet fall to the floor.

The gaze he'd managed to keep to the floor, caught sight of her bare feet and lingered upward on shapely calves. He'd have to have been a blind fool not to notice she had nice legs. Very nice legs.

"I get to start at 8:30, which allows me time to drop Jason off at school and no need for early morning childcare, and we're done at the hotel by four o'clock at the latest on a normal day. Sometimes, during the slower season with a full crew, we're finished even sooner, and I get to pick up Jason earlier." She shifted again and leaned her head back against the cushion, her chin rising just enough to once again expose her neck fully.

Tired of fighting, his mind shot straight to how much he wanted just a small taste of her neck, then her chin, then … "It's late for you. I'd better get going." He couldn't stand up fast enough. If he stayed in her apartment any longer, he was going to forget most of this scenario was just pretend and make a move he knew wasn't smart. No matter how much he wanted it.

"Oh." She popped to her feet. "Yeah. Mornings come around awfully early."

Blast. Did his mind have to take off to what she would look like in the early morning, sleepy eyed and her hair all tousled? He seriously needed to get his butt out of her home. "Thanks for the coffee. I'll see you tomorrow."

"Bright and early." She pulled open the door and stood at the edge, less than a foot away from him. Actually only inches.

"Yes." He moved to cross the threshold when he realized he wasn't quite ready to let go. Stopping short, he spun around to ask her what time she wanted him to pick her up on Saturday. What he hadn't accounted for was her coming around behind him. Instead of finding her a foot or more away, she was right there against him. Her mouth dropped open in surprise, and his instincts kicked in.

His fingers curled around the back of her neck, pulling her nearer. Leaning in, he closed the short distance between them. The zing of electricity that crackled through him the second their lips touched had his other hand pulling her hard against him. What should have been a sweet, easy kiss had turned into a full-blown tangle of lips and a desperate need for more.

Every soft curve of her delicate frame pressed against him from head to toe. Her hands wove around his waist; a low-keyed moan escaped between them, and the fire burning in his blood escalated like a lit match on gasoline. He wanted this woman. Desperately. Mind, body and soul.

"Mommy."

The single word registered in Hope's mind way faster than his. He'd barely processed the loss of her warmth as she sprang away, and he realized Jason had come down the narrow hall, rubbing his sleepy eyes.

"Baby, what are you doing out of bed?"

"I have to go potty." The kid seemed more asleep than awake.

"Okay, honey." She was already walking away from the

door and up the hall when she turned to him. "This will only take a minute."

Brad nodded but knew the best thing he could do was leave. Swallowing hard, he forced the words from his lips. "You take care of him. I'll let myself out."

With her right hand on her son's shoulder, turning him toward the bathroom door, she bobbed her head. "Good night."

"Don't forget to lock up after me." Watching her nod and disappear into the bathroom with her son, he closed the door behind him and stared at the walkway in front of him. One foot in front of the other would get him to his car and then back to his hotel. He'd be peacefully alone and could get some much neglected work done before resuming his pretence tomorrow.

Except, what he really wanted to do right now was turn around and knock on the door. He wanted to help tuck Jason in, to read him a bedtime story, to share another cup of coffee with Hope. And that was only the beginning of what was becoming a very long of list of wants—all including Hope, Jason, and a house with a spacious back yard. And none of which included telling her who he really was and that his stupid acquisition plans would cost her and the other employees much-needed jobs. What kind of mess had he gotten himself into?

CHAPTER NINE

oly hot lips. Hands actually shaking, Hope dumped the rest of the carafe of hot coffee down the sink and poured herself an ice-cold glass of water.

Every nerve ending in her entire body still tingled. From a kiss. One single sensational kiss. Had it been so long that she had completely forgotten how fabulous a kiss could be? Or had no one ever kissed her like *that*? Downing the entire glass in one very long gulp, Hope poured herself another and took a seat on the sofa. Legs curled beneath her, she set the glass on the end table and reached for the remote. She had little doubt she would not be getting much sleep tonight.

Surfing the channels, quickly bypassing anything rated R, she nearly groaned with frustration. What would have happened had Jason not woken up? How far would she have gone? How far would Brad have taken it? He seemed pretty eager to escape. Was he just being a gentleman? Or was the reminder she came with the baggage of a little boy a turnoff? Or had she been such a lousy kisser that he wasn't interested at all?

No. That made no sense. She may not have been kissing a whole lot of guys for a whole lot of time, but *this* guy was most definitely as consumed by the connection as she'd been. And would, no doubt, be again if she got within five feet of Brad Kane. Oh, heavens, and she'd agreed to spend Saturday with him. Well, with him and Jason. In the daytime. Besides, Jason had already proved to be an excellent chaperone. The kid worked better than ice water.

She stood and opened the sofabed. All she needed was to relax and not let her mind run away with all the what-ifs.

After a good night's sleep and with her senses back under control, she'd revisit what happened and decide what to do next—or not to do.

"What on earth are you doing on my doorstep at this hour?" John Maplewood swung open his front door, allowing his best friend inside.

"I've been driving for hours and not getting anywhere."

Ava Maplewood came down the stairs, securing the belt on her bathrobe. "Oh, dear, I'll put on the coffee. This looks like a two-pot night."

Before Brad could say yes or no, Ava had turned toward the kitchen, and John had steered him into living room.

"So what's got you looking like your cat died?" John poured a scotch neat and handed it to Brad. "Drink this before she gets back with the coffee."

Brad downed it in one fast gulp.

John's brows shot up, and that annoying cocky grin slid across his face.

"What?" Brad handed John the empty glass.

"You're the one who texted me that you needed to talk. You tell me."

Rubbing the heel of his palm against his forehead, Brad considered his words. For hours he'd driven up and down the Kona coastline, at first in the cheap rental he'd used with Hope and then in his BMW that he'd missed so much in just a few days. Neither had helped. "I don't know where to start."

"Is this about the hotel? Did something go wrong?"

"No and yes. Or maybe yes and yes. I don't know." Never in his entire life had he felt so confused. Torn.

John didn't say a word. His long time friend simply sat in his favorite leather chair and waited.

"EastCo has a policy that all management must have college degrees."

John nodded.

"It's been in place from day one. Standard for major corporations."

"This is a problem?" John cocked his chin forward.

"Yes. No. Maybe."

"Decisive. Good." Leaning back, John stared stone-faced.

Brad shot him a three fingered salute. "Read between the lines."

"Mature too." John remained unfazed. "We're making progress."

"It's Hope."

A curve at one side of his mouth, John continued to wait.

"She's the head of housekeeping at the hotel."

"And the one with the broken-down car."

"Yes." He waved awkwardly toward the bar and the scotch. "Got another one of those?"

John shook his head. "One takes the edge off. Two won't solve anything. Keep going."

Brad pushed to his feet and walked to the window. "She doesn't have a degree. But she does have an eight-year-old son. Jason. Cute kid."

"The one who wants to play baseball?"

Brad nodded. "Seems pretty smart for eight. At least I think so. She'd have to take a pay cut and go back to cleaning rooms full time when we implement EastCo's policies."

"You are the boss."

That much he knew. He'd already told himself all he had to do was say so, and she'd keep her job. Wouldn't have to know she'd been an exception. And he wouldn't have to dwell over how many other people lost their jobs because of his standard policies. "I gave the hotel employees a thousand-dollar bonus so he could play ball."

"Run that by me again?" John leaned forward again, his eyes wide with surprise.

Brad spun around to face him. "After talking to Ava, I realized she was right. The problem with Hope letting Jason play ball was most likely the money, and Hope does seem to have a hard time accepting help so giving her the money outright probably wouldn't have gone very far. Instead I gave every employee of the hotel a one-thousand-dollar gift. Called it a bonus for staying with us during the transition."

"Did it work?"

"Yeah." He dipped his chin. "We're buying him new gear on Saturday."

"We?" That eyebrow shot up high on his forehead again.

Brad nodded.

John leaned back again. "It's not her job security that has you tied up in knots."

"She doesn't know anything about sports." It was a stupid thing to say, but he didn't want to give voice to what had been spinning around in his head for hours.

"And you don't know anything about eight-year-olds."

Ava came into the room carrying a tray with cups. She looked to her husband. "He's got it?"

"Bad," John deadpanned.

Wincing, she set the tray on the coffee table, then handed Brad a mug of black coffee. "You'd better tell her the truth about who you are sooner than later. And be warned, she'll be pissed." She gave a coffee mug to her husband, then holding her own cup turned back to Brad. "If you need a woman's point of view, let me know."

Both men watched her exit, but John continued to follow her with his eyes long after Brad had turned away.

Ava and John had to be wrong. "It can't be."

John simply stared at him. That all-knowing, all-seeing look that almost always got John his way.

Brad slid into the nearest seat. How could they be right? "I've known the woman all of two days."

A raucous laugh came from John. "I felt like I'd been hit by a sledge hammer the second I saw Ava standing by her brother's car. I was a little slow on the uptake to accept what was happening. Men like us often are. Cynics at heart I guess, but the feeling still hasn't gone away. Call it hokey, call it sappy, call it malarkey, whatever you like. For some people, when it's *the* one, it just is."

"Maybe *it's* just lust."

"Uh-huh." John took a sip of the steaming coffee.

"I mean, it has been a little while."

John balanced his mug on his knee. "In these hours you've been driving around before coming here, did you stop at a night spot? Sleazy or otherwise? Hook up?"

"No." The thought hadn't even occurred to him. He didn't want to pick up any woman. He wanted Hope.

John shook his head and raised his mug stopping short at his lips. "Any more questions?"

Sitting on the edge of his seat, his forearms resting on his thighs, Brad looked up at his most trusted friend. "Yeah. What do I do now?"

CHAPTER TEN

For two days Hope had been on pins and needles. She'd seen Brad in passing. A wave or a nod. Never close enough to talk and she had no reason to search him out. She often went days without seeing senior management. Heck, the only reason she saw as much of Keith as she did was because he'd always found reasons to come to her.

Now she was wondering if Brad might be dodging her altogether. Another reason why she'd avoided getting involved with a man all these years. For the same two days she'd been reliving that world-altering kiss, Jason had been talking about nothing else but going shopping with Brad tomorrow. She couldn't even fathom how she would deal with her son's disappointment if Brad backed out.

"How's it going?" Keith appeared in her doorway.

"It's going." She tried to plaster on a cheery smile until she took a longer look into Keith's eyes. "What's wrong?"

Easing his way into the tiny office, he moved a stack of paper off the only other chair available, dropped it on the floor, and scooted the seat closer to the desk before sitting.

Her stomach felt as though a swarm of angry bees had made themselves at home. Whatever the heck was wrong, was *very* wrong.

"I got the paperwork on the two maids EastCo is transferring to us from the other side of the island."

"And?"

"They seem fine. Nothing unusual. They're actually experienced maids. Were with the Royal Palms even before EastCo bought them out."

She really wished he would get to the part that had him

pulling up a chair to talk to her.

"Attached to the employee files were EastCo's HR descriptions of their jobs. You know, experience required and all the other crap which comes with the hiring process."

Crap? Now she knew she wasn't going to like what he had to say.

"There was also the description and qualifications for your job."

Okay, that did it. Her stomach was now officially under attack. The score, Hope zero, bees two.

Keith leaned forward. "Hope, I don't know how to tell you this other than to just spit it out. At EastCo, all managerial positions require a degree. A college degree."

"And I don't have one." No need to read between the lines. The writing on the wall was in large bold print. As soon as this transition to EastCo was complete, she would be screwed out of her job.

Today was Brad's turn on the grounds crew. On a scale of one to ten, it was somewhere above facilities, otherwise known as janitorial, and under reservations. He wouldn't have minded slapping a guest or two upside the head. The patience his people had to show while talking to disrespectful adults—who wouldn't be happy until they got an oceanfront room for the price of a popsicle—was mind-boggling.

The only good thing about baking under the Hawaiian sun was he got to see a lot more of the comings and goings of the staff. Like why the heck was his hotel manager heading toward the same building that officed housekeeping? It had become pretty obvious to him by Keith's oddly protective behavior that, rather than maintaining good order at the workplace, what Keith had was a thing for Hope.

Perched on the end of his rake, he came within seconds of checking out what was going on for himself. For two days he'd forced himself to stay away from Hope. Convinced that, if he could escape the physical connection, he'd get his head screwed on straight and be able to think more rationally. There was nothing rational about the way he felt at this moment. *Territorial* didn't even begin to cover it. *Assault and battery* came close. *Murder* was more in the ballpark. And then he saw Keith leaving. Not that much can happen in—he looked at his watch—a fifteen-minute visit. At least not if the guy knew what he was doing.

Moving the same small pile of leaves back and forth at his feet, he kept his eyes on Keith until the man was once again in the main hotel building. Shoving aside the pile with one angry broad stroke, Brad would have smacked himself if he could. Talk about overreacting. He had no claim on Hope and no reason to believe anything was going on between her and Keith. Even if there were, none of it was his business. But that was the kick of it. He wanted it to be his business. Very much.

John was right. It is what it is. Brad could hide from his growing feelings as long as he wanted, but that didn't change the fact that Hope had made herself at home under his skin. He had no idea if it was her pretty smile, her sense of loyalty to the company, her concern for her coworkers, her love for her son, or the way she nibbled on her lower lip every time she worried about money. But, whatever the heck it was, he wanted more of it. "Henry."

"Yes, boss man?"

Brad almost laughed. Today he was just part of the crew, but the other guy assigned to the same detail still treated him like a hotel manager. If the guy knew who he really was, he'd have a cow. "I'm taking a break. Getting a drink. Want something?"

"No thanks." Henry pointed to the water bottle at his side. "I'm fine."

"Be right back." Brad wished he weren't so sweaty, but enough was enough. He needed to at least check in on Hope. If nothing else, he had the perfect excuse—confirming tomorrow's shopping date.

Stopping in the men's room just inside the doorway, he took a second to wash his hands and face and do a fast finger-comb of his hair. Looking in the mirror, he decided his appearance could be a lot worse. By later this afternoon he'd be stinking like a wet dog.

"You got a minute?" He rapped on the door frame and almost leapt into the room when she raised her head, and he found those beautiful green eyes were laced red from crying. He was definitely going to murder Keith, preferably slowly and painfully.

She bowed her head, returning to the paperwork in front of her. "Not now. I'm behind on the laundry report."

To hell with laundry. Ignoring her, he stepped into the room and closed the door behind him. "What happened? Is it Jason?"

Her head shot up. "Oh, no." The back of her hand swiped at an escaped tear. "He's fine. I'm just not taking some difficult news well."

So it was Keith. What had the ass-hat done? "I've been told I'm a good listener."

She ran another hand under her other eye. Straightening in her seat, she sucked in a deep breath, put on a brave smile, and he knew as sure as his name was Bradford Peyton that he was, beyond any doubt, falling in love with the woman in front of him.

"Thanks, but I'll be fine," she answered. "What did you need?"

To know what that idiot said to you. "What time did you want me to pick you up tomorrow?" For a moment he thought he saw a tiny spark of pleasure peek out from behind those sad eyes. Or was it just wishful thinking on his part?

"It's up to you." She forced a feeble smile.

"Nine o'clock too early?"

This time her eyes definitely lit briefly with amusement. "I have an eight-year-old. What do you think?"

That he didn't have a clue was the first thing to come to mind and that he didn't care came second. "Nine o'clock it is. And ... well, if you tell me what's bothering you, maybe

I can help."

She shook her head and pressed her lips together as though that might still the tears once again pooling in her eyes. Taking a deep breath and blowing it out slowly, her shoulders seemed to deflate with the expelled breath. "I was lucky that the Paradise Shores' former owner believed there was no substitute for hard work and experience"

He nodded. The owner, Brad was learning, was much smarter than he'd given the guy credit for.

Her eyes fell shut again. "Not even a college degree."

A nasty knot formed in the pit of his stomach.

Breathing in and out again, she leveled her gaze with his. "It appears EastCo doesn't follow the same philosophy."

"They didn't fire you, did they?" They couldn't have. He clearly told his assistant to hold back the transition phase of Paradise Shores.

"No." She snatched a pen from the desk and rolled it between her fingers. "But it won't be long."

"You're good at your job. You care. Don't hesitate to step in and do the work yourself if needed. That's a rare commodity in an employee."

"Tell that to EastCo."

That's exactly what he had in mind. "Listen, try not to worry. I have a lot of friends in the business. I'm sure something will work out."

She smiled up at him. "You're a very sweet man, Brad. A bit of an optimist but sweet." Scooting closer to her desk, she waved him away. "You'd better get back to work before we both wind up getting the ax."

Right about now, the need to assure her all would be well almost had him telling her the truth about himself, to hell with the stupid two-week challenge. But an even stronger gut instinct told him, if he shared his secret now, he wouldn't stand an ice cube's chance in the sun of getting the girl. "You're right, but I'll check in on you later."

Still smiling, she nodded at him.

Outside the building he glanced around and walked toward the empty beach. Cell phone in hand he hit speed dial to his office. "Carol."

"How's today going?"

"To hell in a handbasket."

"What do I need to do?" This was why Carol was worth her weight to him in gold. No hurt feelings, just ready to man the battle stations.

"Listen very carefully. I want the following change written into policies for every last damn department in every damn division of EastCo. From now on, all internal applicants for executive and managerial positions can substitute on-the-job and life experience to fulfill degree requirements. Then get legal to give you the right mumbo jumbo to grandfather-in all positions from acquired companies, regardless of qualifications criteria, without us getting stuck with the crackpots. Got it?"

"Do you want me to tell legal exactly that?"

"Tell them anything you want, including, if I don't have this back and enforceable by end of business tomorrow, they can all find new jobs."

"Yes, sir. Got it." If anyone could prod legal into actually pulling this together in twenty four hours, it was Carol.

Shoving his phone into his pocket, Brad stomped back to his job for the day. Ava had been right. Being the one to buy the new toy was one thing, but having to polish it first yourself made one helluva difference. EastCo was in for some major changes when he got back to his office. And John was right too about Hope. She was *it* for Brad, but how to get her to fall for Bradford Peyton was something he had no clue how to do. Or did he?

CHAPTER ELEVEN

Tears welled in Hope's eyes. It was silly. Mothers weren't supposed to cry watching their sons play catch. Though she knew darn well it wasn't Jason throwing the ball that had her all misty, but the man squatting in front of him showing him how to catch with a mitt.

As she'd expected, there was nothing special or complicated about sports shopping for a little boy. They'd bought socks and shorts and left the jersey so the store could imprint his team name and number. Brad had insisted on buying the mitt as a gift, and, though Hope had almost stopped breathing at the price tag on the glove he'd chosen, Brad had instantly put her at ease.

"I'm single, well-employed, and have nothing else to spend my money on. Let me get him a good glove."

And she had. She'd also let him buy a batting practice set so he could help Jason with his swing before the official practices started. From where she sat on the park bleachers, Brad was going to have a lot of instruction time ahead of him.

"Hi there." Kara Harper climbed onto the bleacher beside her. "I thought it was you up here."

Hope didn't see anyone else. "Are you alone?"

"No. Nick and Bradley are getting the gear from the car. Catherine is with her grandmother. Well, sort of her grandmother." Kara chuckled to herself. "Long story for another day."

Something Kara's easy manner made Hope want to hear the long story. Maybe some day. She had never really had time to make friends with parents or have play dates like so many families with two parents. She looked to the field where Nick and Bradley and another man were sauntering up to where Jason and Brad were. "I'm sure we won't stay much longer."

"Nonsense. Baseball is a team sport. It'll be good for everyone to get some practice in. The men love this sort of thing. That fella there, that's Doug. He's married to a friend of mine. They haven't any children." Kara turned to her and smiled. "Yet—but he volunteers to coach and loves it. He's coming off basketball with some special needs kids and promised Nick he'd help with Bradley's team."

"Oh," Hope looked down at the massive amount of bags and equipment Nick and the others had unloaded. "I didn't realize Nick was the coach."

"Yep," Kara laughed. "I'm lucky that the price of this boy's toys doesn't get any higher than a few bats, and gloves, and shoes, and," she laughed some more. "you see where I'm going with this."

After shopping with Brad and his penchant for the pricier toys, she easily laughed with her new friend. She really did get it. For the next while they chatted about anything from how fast kids grow to the price of gasoline to how to get paint off the kids' clothes. By the time she got the full story on her husband Nick's best friend's mother stepping in as a grandmother figure, Hope was laughing so hard at the stories, she ached for a big happy family to fuss with.

"I think those guys are having too much fun." Kara pointed to the field.

The men were laughing, switching places between batting and base coaches as each of the boys took turns and ran around the diamond. Plenty of high fives were shared, but more amongst the adults than the kids. Hope had to agree, the guys seemed to be bonding as much as she and Kara were. Which was really nice. She felt as though she'd made a new friend. Even though Kara was a part time attorney, and Hope was a glorified maid, she felt like she and Jason fit right in with the Harpers. And she liked it.

"Looks like the boys are packing up." Kara pointed to

her husband, collecting balls into a bag.

"Yeah, it's time for lunch. They're probably starved."

Jason came running up and onto the bleachers, his friend on his heels. "Mommy, Mommy." At the top he practically crashed into her. "Can I go play at Bradley's house?"

Bradley sidled up by his mom. "Dad said it was okay."

"I don't know," Hope supplied. She wouldn't have wanted something like that sprung on her.

"Please. Please," the two boys echoed.

"We could bring him home later if you'd like?" Kara offered. "It's no problem. The more the merrier. It will be nice for Bradley and Jason to hang out."

And to play in a backyard, Hope thought. Until now she'd not let Jason accept any invitations to play at the homes of the other kids, afraid of what he'd feel about not having what they had. Now she realized how unfair she'd been to him. "Sure. Just call me when I need to come pick him up."

"Yay!" The boys ran off, shouting to the men waiting below.

Hope pulled out her phone. "What's your number?" Their telephone numbers exchanged, Hope climbed down to meet up with Brad. "I guess I've lost my son for the rest of the day."

"How about an early lunch? I know a great little place to eat by the shore—"

"Oh, you don't have to ..." A huge smile pulled at her cheeks. "Sounds delicious."

They'd barely made it out of the parking lot when her cell phone sounded. "Hello?"

"Sorry to bother you—" Nina was on the other end "—but Teresa called in sick, and Sofia just sliced her hand open and is on her way to the ER, and we're way behind."

"And you called everyone else?"

"Yeah, sorry."

"All right. I'll pick up my car and be right over."

"A couple of hours and we should be caught up. I won't need you to stay till we're all done."

"No problem. See you soon." Normally when she had to fill in for a few hours on a busy weekend, she'd just bring Jason with her and make the best of it. There was no making the best of losing out on a seaside lunch with Brad.

"They're calling you in on your day off?" Brad kept his eyes on the road.

"It happens. If you'll just drop me off at home, I'll pick up my car."

Instead of turning right at the corner toward her house, Brad turned left. "I'll take you. Four hands will be better than two."

"This time I have to say it. You don't have to do that."

He cracked a cocky smile. "Yeah, I do. I'm higher up on the food chain than you are. If it's your responsibility to run and help, it's even more so mine."

"Maybe, but still …"

"Besides, together we'll knock out the work faster, and then we can have a late lunch."

Her cheeks tugged at the corner of her mouth. "I like the sound of that."

"A late lunch?"

She nodded, but what really made her toes tingle and her face want to burst into a happy grin was the word *together*. Having someone to count on, no matter what, was looking way better than nice. So far, Brad had proved her wrong. He had plenty of substance.

Who would have thought coaching a handful of elementary school kids could be fun? When Jason finally swung and hit the ball, Brad was almost more excited than Jason. Brad actually found himself thinking ahead to spending more time with the boy—and his mother. Without trying, Brad could see them in a house with a big yard and a younger brother or sister in a family-size SUV. And wasn't that tidbit of information going to make his mother a happy woman?

Stopping at the red light, he faced the woman who had come to mean so much to him in such a short time. "Listen, later, at lunch ..."

"Yes?" Oh, how her eyes sparkled in the sunlight.

He swallowed hard. Telling her the truth would never get any easier. It had to be done, and he was pretty sure that once again in this case, Ava would be right. Sooner would be better than later. "I've got a few things I'd like to share with you."

"Like what?"

"Not now. We're almost at the hotel, and I don't want to be interrupted." And didn't want her any place she could walk away from him before he could make her see how important she and Jason were to him.

"It's not bad news, is it?" Her brows formed a fretful V. "You're not trying to butter me up or something?"

"No." At least he hoped not. He had already started praying Hope wouldn't be put off by his interference and subterfuge at the hotel. "I'm hoping you'll think it's good news."

Nodding and smiling again, she leaned back into the seat. "Then I guess I'll wait."

And she was doing a better job of it then he was. As a businessman, he knew how to bide his time, but when it came to Hope, he seemed to have a hard time being patient. He pulled into the hotel parking lot and almost bit his lip to keep from pulling her into his arms for a quick kiss.

Inside the hotel they worked side by side. Getting time alone with her enough motivation for him to move at lightening speed. But even with two of them working as fast as they could cleaning rooms, they were still lagging behind from where they needed to be.

He, Hope, and a girl named Lani were working the same floor but not making much progress.

"Does she always work so slowly?" Brad had restocked their carts twice already and Lani had yet to request a restock.

"Some days are better than others." Hope shrugged and snapped the fresh sheet onto the newly stripped bed.

It struck him that he'd heard this woman's name before. "Hope, are you covering for her?"

"Everyone has hard times." She averted his gaze and tucked the bottom sheet in at one corner.

Brad moved to the foot of the bed and reached for the other end of the sheet. "You're not answering my question."

"And I'm not going to. My people are my problem." She shifted to another corner.

"Then she is a problem?" He closed the gap, coming up directly behind her. When she stiffened, he took hold of her in his hands and spun her about to face him. "Who else do you cover for?"

"No one." She closed her eyes and sucked in a deep breath, slowly blowing it out before meeting his gaze. "Lani has three kids under six, and a boyfriend who shows up long enough to get her pregnant, take what money she's saved, and disappear again. She's totally reliable and dependable when he's not around. I think he's back, but I can't get her to talk to me."

Hope was as beautiful inside as she was out. He knew he shouldn't, but he brushed a stray lock of hair from across her cheek and tucked it behind her ear. "Covering for her isn't going to fix her boyfriend problems."

"Maybe not. But firing her isn't going to fix anything either." The sparkle in her eyes had turned to fire. She was like a mama lion protecting her cub. This woman was amazing. So many problems of her own on the forefront but she was fighting for someone who clearly couldn't fight for herself. Neither of them had moved. They still stood toe to toe. Chest to chest.

Resisting the urge to kiss the chin tilted up in determination, Brad nodded. "No. You're right. But there has to be some agency that can help. I'll look into it."

"I've tried." Some of the fight slipped away from her. "Lani won't cooperate. I keep hoping something will change." Her gaze fixed on his, she slipped her tongue out to moisten her lower lip, and all the blood in his veins rushed south.

"Do you have any idea how special you are?" This

wasn't the time or place to get personal. He knew that more than anyone. But he couldn't resist one quick tiny peck on the lips.

Except there was no such thing as tiny or quick when it came to his mouth on Hope. The slightest taste and he wanted more. Just like the other night, within seconds, heat spread through him, hot and scorching like flames on kerosene.

"Brad," she mumbled against his lips, her breath warm and taunting.

His lips eased away from hers, trailing kisses across her jaw. "Oh, Hope."

"Yes," she muttered softly.

For a long frozen second Brad stared down at her. "God, you are beautiful." He didn't dare share everything he thought and felt for fear she'd think him crazy. Crazy in love.

CHAPTER TWELVE

Hope's cell phone sounded off. "Someone probably needs more sheets."

He could stare at her like this in his arms for the rest of his life. "Ignore them. Maybe they'll go away."

"I doubt it," she mumbled, her hand pressed flat against his chest she just wanted to feel his strength below her fingertips another moment.

Dipping his chin, his forehead came to rest on hers. "You have no idea how much I want to just give them our cart and stay right here where we are."

Oh, yeah, she had a pretty good idea. Too bad a nervous edge was building in her gut. This was all happening so fast, and she was liking it too much. Pulling completely away she reached for her phone before it went to voice mail. "Hello?"

"Good news," Nina's voice echoed on speaker. "We're just about caught up. Call this your last room and turn the works over to Lani."

Stepping back, she brushed her hand nervously along her slacks. "Thanks, Nina. We're almost done here."

She'd barely disconnected when, brushing the back of his knuckles along her chin, Brad leaned into her again. "When we're done here we'll pick up some food and go some place quiet to have that talk I mentioned earlier."

"Food sounds great." Using a smile to camouflage her concerns, she shoved any misgivings to the back of her mind. Whatever news he had to share, she wasn't going to let her imagination ruin how fabulous she felt at this very moment. Whatever she and Brad had, she was going to enjoy every minute of it for as long as she could. Even if it meant risking another broken heart.

She shifted to move around him, but Brad ran his fingers along her arm. Catching hold of her hand, he quickly squeezed before letting go, and she grinned like a besotted schoolgirl. Yeah, she was definitely on board for whatever this man had to offer.

The beds made, and the bathroom cleaned, Brad opened the door to the hall and had barely gotten the cart out when an angry shout caught his attention. Backing out of the room, he strained to hear the muffled sounds of what he thought was a female voice followed by a much louder male voice.

"That doesn't sound good." Hope craned her neck to see up the hall.

Hairs on the back of Brad's neck came to full attention. Parking the cart to the side of the hall, he moved briskly in the direction of the argument. Hurrying faster as the voices grew louder and more agitated, he listened carefully. Several rooms away, a door flew open.

"Where'd you effing put it?"

The cracking echo of a hand across flesh ripped through Brad and sent him into a full gallop, rapidly swallowing the short distance remaining between him and the woman's cries.

"I didn't hide it. I paid the rent," the frazzled voice cried.

"Lying bi..."

"Hey." Cutting the man off, Brad screeched to halt. In front of him was a petite woman, her back pressed to the wall, one hand cradling her cheek, the other hand remained protectively over her stomach. He'd also come face-to-face with a bear of a man, standing, arm raised. Poised to strike again. "I wouldn't do that if I were you."

Bear Man turned and growled out, "Mind your own business," as he pushed at the door to slam it closed.

Brad caught the door and shoved it open all the way.

"Not happening."

A fire burned strong in the man's eyes. The guy was either high as a kite or truly a madman.

For Brad, it didn't matter which. "Step away from her."

"I'm calling 9-1-1," Hope yelled from the hall. Other guests must have come from their rooms, as Brad could hear the din of low murmurs behind him.

"We don't need no cops. And we don't need you. This is a family matter."

"Not in my hotel it's not." Brad spread his feet slightly for better balance. One of two things was about to happen: this character would get a flash of wisdom and take off for safer ground, or he would start swinging. Either way, Brad was ready for him.

"What's going on?" Out of breath, Keith rushed up behind Brad.

"This gentleman was just about to leave before the police arrive."

That was all the additional motivation the nutcase needed. Letting out another bestial roar, the guy lunged at Brad. Anticipating the move, Brad shifted his weight and threw a punch. In seconds they were both on the ground. Keith, unprepared for the assault, was knocked back into the hall. A woman screamed behind him, maybe more than one. Running steps could be heard in the hall. The cops or security.

Either way it didn't matter. High on drugs, a brute this size would have taken half a dozen men to hold him down. But up close and personal, Bearman here wreaked of too much liquor. It took Brad all of fifteen seconds to flip the idiot and pin him facedown to the ground. With Brad's knee pressing all his weight into the guy's shoulder blades and restraining both his arms behind his back, Bearman wasn't going anywhere of his own free will anytime soon.

Hotel security came up behind him.

"Do you have handcuffs?" Brad asked.

"Yes, sir." The young kid, built like a linebacker, kneeled beside Brad and, biting back a smile, slipped the cuffs onto the guy's wrists and jerked him to his feet.

Brad was pretty sure this was the most fun this security guard had ever had. "Take this creep out front. Cops should be here any minute."

"You okay?" Keith scanned Brad as he pushed to his feet.

Brad brushed himself off and tucked in his shirttail. "Fine."

"Good. I'll go with security to meet the cops. You all right with handling everything in here?"

"Yeah. Fine. Go. And let the police know I am most definitely pressing charges."

Keith nodded, and he and security escorted the still-growling man down the hall.

"Sorry for any inconvenience," Brad addressed the few guests standing warily in the hall.

One guy about his size and a few years older walked over and offered his hand to Brad. "I would have stepped in to help, but you seemed to have it under control pretty fast. Good job."

"My mom will be thrilled to know all those years in high school spent getting knocked senseless as a running back paid off."

The other guy laughed at the football joke, then turned and ushered his wife into their room.

Brad had a feeling he was about to meet Lani. Spinning around to the woman still in the room, he was relieved to see her standing, shoulders straight. "You'll need some ice for that," he said.

Her hand drifted again to her cheek as she shook her head. "Thank you. And I'm really sorry. I never thought he'd come to work."

"You have nothing to apologize for. The problem is all his. And he can stew over it from the inside of a jail cell."

"He's not always like this." A wistful expression fell over her face.

Brad couldn't imagine a nice side to the guy he'd just wrestled with. "If you need any more help, a lawyer, whatever, just let me know."

"Yes, and thank you again, Mr. Peyton. You really are a good guy."

Shaking his head, he waved off the comment. "I'm just glad I was here."

"So am I. If you don't mind," she shimmied around him. "I have to finish my rooms."

He didn't like the darkening pink on her face. "I think you should take the afternoon off. Get that chin checked out. Make sure he didn't do more serious damage."

"Maybe later. Hope has covered for me enough. I can finish."

"For me," he smiled at her, "would you at least take a few minutes and go put some ice on that?"

Nodding at him, Lani stepped around him, and the last few seconds of conversation suddenly slapped him upside the head. Spinning around, he saw Hope, standing within earshot, her mouth slightly open, her eyes round with surprise, and he feared, *understanding.*

Crap.

Mr. Peyton. Brad Kane. Bradford Peyton. It couldn't be. But there was no mistaking that Lani called him Mr. Peyton and he didn't correct her. He'd also told her husband *not in his hotel. His.* Dear Lord, she'd just locked lips and come seriously close to so much more with the new CEO of the hotel. No. That couldn't be. How? There had to be a mistake. If she thought chances for anything permanent were slim before, what chance did a glorified maid with a young kid have with a jet setting billionaire?

"Lani." Hope snapped herself out of a pity fest and turned and followed the battered woman away from the room. She could have a well deserved cry later. "Are you okay?"

The other woman nodded. "I'm getting some ice. Then I'll be back. Thank heaven Mr. Peyton was here."

"Yes, you said that before. How do you know him?"

"Oh, before I worked here, I worked at the Royal Palm. Whenever Mr. Peyton was in town, he would stay there. Such a good looking man. And a nice smile. I'd always heard nice things about him, but he was the last person I expected to find here in the hall. I guess it makes sense, now that his company owns the Paradise Shores."

"Yes." Her luck had just run out. "It makes sense."

Lani turned toward the infirmary, and Hope found herself walking directly to the back door. Somewhere behind her she heard her name. *Brad.* She picked up the pace, determined to get out of here. Shoving the door with all she had, she practically ran from the building and down the path.

"Hope! Stop," Brad called after her.

No. Not now. *Why?* Without further thought she raced past the main building and into the lot where all the employees parked. Lined against the wall were a myriad of vehicles. Sedans, SUVs, pickups, all of them older models, none of them hers.

Brad ran up beside her, breathing heavy from the mad dash. "Hope."

"I don't have my car." Hugging her arms, she could think of nothing else to say. She didn't want to break down here in front of everyone and she didn't want to face him. Not now, not yet.

"We came in mine." He pushed the key fob and the white car beeped. "We'll get something to eat. I'll explain."

Being stranded in the parking lot with little choice as to where to go, she turned to face him—still drowning in her own thoughts, a shimmer of anger replacing the hurt. "What's to explain? You're a rich hotel magnate, and I'm head of housekeeping." Her fisted hands landed on her hips. "And you lied to me."

"Not to you. Well"—he raked his fingers through his hair and blew out a big breath—"it was a dare."

"Which part? The lie? Or kissing me, making me think that maybe…" Her words trailed off. She was quickly going from hurt and confused to seriously ticked off.

"Working undercover in my own company. I turned down the TV show, and my friends challenged me to do it anyway."

"What?" Of all the possible explanations, that wasn't anywhere near what she'd expected. Who uses a TV show as an excuse for crappy behavior?

He reached for her, then thinking better of it, shoved his hands in his pockets. "My friend's wife, a very smart woman by the way, said you wouldn't like it when you found out about me. Anyhow, she's the one originally who insisted I would learn more about my company, working here as an equal, than from reading reports. And she was right about that too."

Was he serious? "Any idiot could have told you that."

"Are you calling me an idiot?" A hint of a smile teased at the corner of his mouth.

She wasn't the least bit amused. "If you're telling me the truth, then yes."

He went from amused to stunned in nothing flat. He stood quietly a moment, and then, with an assenting dip of his head, he shrugged one shoulder. "I guess I am about a lot of things. But do I get any grace for being a fast learner and wanting to tell you the truth?"

"The road to hell is paved with good intentions." She shifted and crossed her arms.

"That may be, but I specifically told you that I had something to tell you. Twice."

Her mouth fell open prepared to bark back, when her brain cells kicked in. He had. Her jaw snapped shut and her arms fell to her sides. He'd mentioned something to tell her both before and later …

"See. You're starting to believe me. I'm a nice guy. Really I am. And I can learn to be nicer. Or at least smarter." He moved closer to her, and she resisted the urge to step back. "I know ignorance is no excuse." He pulled one hand slowly from his pocket and fingered a lock of hair fallen lose from the bun she'd pinned to the back of her head. "But I couldn't have possibly known I would fall in love with a total stranger in just a few days."

This time she leaned forward, not so much from will but sheer imbalance. Her world was quickly spinning out of control. "You … what?"

"It took me two days to realize I loved you and another two days to accept the truth. All I ask of you now is to give us time for you to fall in love with me. You already like me. And I'm really the same guy, just with a pretty hefty bank account and a stupid sports car."

"Stupid?"

"Can't haul baseball equipment and kids around in a sports car. I'll get an SUV."

He was talking kids and baseball. Was it foolish that her heart was swelling in her chest? That she wanted to believe him? Desperately wanted to believe him?

A sparkle twinkled in his eyes. "We'll keep the BMW for just the two of us, once in a while."

Oh, Lord, she was so out of her league. "I don't—"

"Let's start with lunch. You and me. We'll talk about normal things. Everyday things. Baseball."

There was so much hope and desperation staring back at her. Could this be real? Could the man she'd fallen in love with like a princess in a fairy tale really love her back? Was there a happy-ever-after ending in this crazy scenario? Her head bobbed, and slowly a smile tugged her cheeks into a face-splitting grin. "Yes." *Damn it, yes.* "I'd love to have lunch with you." And maybe something more.

The next thing she knew, she'd been sucked into a bone-crushing embrace and lifted high into the air, her feet dangling behind her. Brad spun her around, then slid her slowly back down, capturing her mouth in a deal-sealing kiss. "I love you, Hope."

His words had her heart pounding, and sheer joy effervescing from deep inside. "It may not be as hard to make me love you as you think." Her lips met his for a chaste peck. "But," she continued, "there's one thing I still don't get."

"What's that?"

"You said it took you two days to accept the truth. What truth?"

His gaze softened, and her heart melted a little more. "When it's right, it just is."

CHAPTER THIRTEEN

"That's it. Easy on the grip," John called to his nephew from his post at the grille.

Brad and the other adults on the back patio chuckled at the sight of Jason and Bradley teaching Izzy and Catherine how to play T-ball.

The first few weeks after the hotel showdown had been an unexpected challenge for Brad. From the beginning he knew he needed more than money to win Hope over. Not very surprising, his best weapon and ally had turned out to be Ava Maplewood followed by just about every member of the down to earth Everrett clan. But Ava made the most difference. She brought the concept of balance and normal to being married to a man raised with a silver spoon in his mouth and had put Hope instantly at ease. From there the two had quickly become fast friends.

Standing beside John, at the grill, Billy Everrett continued to watch the children in the yard. "I think you've got a natural-born athlete."

"Thank you," both Nick and Brad answered in perfect chorus.

It still surprised Brad to realize Nick Harper was practically part of the Everrett clan. Having only met Billy and Angela on his quick visits to the island, he'd only heard of Nick and Doug, and all the others, but had failed to make the connection at the pizza parlor or the field. After all it wasn't really *that* small an island.

Having Nick and his wife and the other Everrett sibling Emily and her husband drop by hadn't been planned. This Saturday afternoon gathering had started out as just Brad and Hope and Jason over at John and Ava's, but somehow when word got out that John was actually manning the grill himself, the small backyard event had turned into an event worthy of the matriarch, Maile Everrett.

"Oh," Doug lifted his chin in the direction of the rear parking lot. "Didn't know Lexi and Jim were in town."

The tall willowy blonde holding hands with a man cut from the same cloth as the other sailors in the family approached. Sporting broad grins and enthusiastic waves, they clearly belonged. For a split moment Brad wondered if there was anyone on the island who didn't belong. Whichever the case, they'd clearly been drinking the same water as everyone else at the impromptu barbecue because he could feel the sizzle in their gazes clear across the yard.

Nick turned and gave a short wave to the couple stopped mid stride by none other than the family matriarch. From the hugs ensued Brad wasn't sure if they hadn't seen each other in quite some time or if it was in the matriarch's job description to ensure everyone's spines were properly aligned.

"Whatever you three are grinning about, the answer is no." Ava set a clean plate in front of her husband, patted his backside, and then spun about to return to the huddle of women across the yard.

John's grin split wide open. "Just doing as my beautiful wife instructed."

Shaking her head and laughing, she shouted over her shoulder. "Flattery will get you everywhere."

The men chuckled and it was obvious to any fool observing all these men were extremely happy.

"Glad to see you're joining the rank and file, Brad." Billy tipped his beer in Hope's direction. "Looks like it was worth the wait."

Brad didn't stop the grin that took over his face. "Definitely." He couldn't imagine going back to a life without Hope. This morning he'd picked out a ring. After all, what made sense three months ago, still made sense today. *When it's right, it just is.* Tonight, after this afternoon's not so little gathering, he was taking her and Jason to the beach for a sunset stroll. And a proposal.

"Okay, guys." Hope sidled up beside Brad and looped her arm around his waist. "Ravenous mothers over here. How much longer?"

"Just another minute or two." John stabbed at another piece of meat.

Doug raised his arm and Ava's sister Emily slid underneath, curling into his side. He'd heard the story of how Doug had accidentally fallen for his best friend's little sister, but judging by the fire in their eyes, he decided Ava was right. It wouldn't be long before they added to Maile Everett's requests for more grandchildren.

"Ava tells me," Emily looked to Brad, "that your bringing a satellite home office to Kona?"

Nodding, Brad tightened his hold on Hope's hip. "We'll be all moved in next week."

"So glad the old dog can learn new tricks from *real* people." Ava settled in beside her husband.

"Is she ever going to let me forget that?" Brad directed his question at John.

"Nope," Ava and Hope responded in unison, then burst into chuckles.

"Admit it," Ava continued. "You learned so much more than you expected to when you took John's challenge."

"I heard it was very *eventful*," Billy casually dropped an arm around his wife who had joined the group. "Your own version of *Undercover CEO*. Quite an eye-opener."

"I recommend every business owner should try it. Including you two."

"Hey," Nick tipped his beer bottle at Brad, "we're already in the thick of things. No stuffy desk jobs for us. Now John here…"

"So not happening." John waved him off, shaking his head, poked at a steak, and nodding satisfaction, dropped it onto an empty plate.

Nick laughed and turned to face Brad. "Have you made any changes yet based on all these eye-opening discoveries?"

"Quite a few." More than Brad could remember at the moment. "After my lead teams got over the shock of being sent into the trenches for a week to learn the nuts and bolts of what's really going on, the list of change recommendations tripled from my initial suggestions."

"And were implemented rather quickly," Hope added.

"I like how you've given your employees access to free legal advice and aid if necessary." John slid the last steak onto the platter. "I like to think I pay all my people well, but heaven knows how many people there are at FJM Global who can't afford good legal advice. I'd hate to think anyone of them would find themselves in a situation like your employee who couldn't keep her dangerous deadbeat ex out of her life."

"True." Billy turned with his wife to follow John and the food.

"It was good of you and your lawyers to take care of Lani's problems and make them available for anyone else at EastCo." Ava paused to call the children to the table, then turned back to Brad. "Trust me when I say, not enough people get involved in domestic abuse cases."

Brad nodded. Truth was, he wished he could do more to help all the Lanis in the world. For now, it was enough to know he'd done all he could for her and her children.

Jason came running up to the table with the other kids in tow and frowned at the large platter of steaks. Before he could say a word, Hope uncovered the plate of cheeseburgers, and the boy's face lit up like the proverbial Christmas tree.

Oh, how Brad loved seeing this kid smile. It had never occurred to him that he could come to love and want to protect one little boy so easily. And, if there was a God in heaven, tonight he, Hope, and her son would be officially on the way to becoming a family.

Hope loved hanging out with Ava and John Maplewood. Who knew that such wealthy and powerful couple were pretty much just people. Ava had quickly helped Hope see that she had no valid reason not to let Brad into her life. The fact that she had struggled all her life and that Brad had had all the advantages didn't mean a thing.

"Here we are." Brad pulled into the parking lot nearest the sea wall. "Time to walk off all those calories."

"And get ice cream," Jason chimed in.

Brad laughed. "And get ice cream."

For a few seconds, while Brad made his way around the car to open her door and then Jason's, Hope lingered in this perfect moment. She didn't want to think about how empty her world would feel if Brad weren't a part of it.

"Come on." Holding out his hand to her, Brad grabbed on tight and didn't let go.

They walked to the shoreline, Jason rambling on at Brad's side about teaching the girls to play ball and how soon soccer season was coming up and Bradley's Uncle Doug had promised to coach both Jason and Bradley. Hope chose to simply enjoy the moment. A short crop of rocks jutted out toward the sea, and Jason pulled away from Brad and ran ahead.

Brad tugged at her hand to trot after him. "Be careful, buddy. No climbing on the big rocks."

"Yeah, well, that just took all the fun out of it." Hope elbowed Brad, knowing full well she was about to say the exact same thing, only he beat her to it.

Brad squeezed her hand and sent all the blood pumping to her heart. How had she grown to love this man so darn much in such a short time? At the foot of the rocks, Brad let go and climbed up to where Jason had stopped. "Remember what you and I talked about?"

Jason nodded.

"Good." Brad grabbed Jason's hand and walked him back to the base of the rocks, where Hope stood watching. Reaching out to her, he directed her to sit on one of the larger rocks, then encouraged Jason to sit beside her.

"What's this all about?" she asked.

"It's a surprise." Jason flashed a toothy grin.

"That's right." Brad stepped right in front of her.

She had no idea what this production was about, but,

holding on tightly to her hand, Brad remained standing.

"I know we haven't been together very long, and we still have a lot to learn about each other, but there's one thing I know for sure. You are the only woman for me. You make me a better man, and I never want to face another day of my life without you at my side. I love you more than words can say and promise to prove that to you every day of your life, if you will do me the honor and joy of becoming my wife."

All the air in her lungs had stopped flowing. Could she possibly have heard him right?

Brad dropped to one knee. "Hope Anne Gibbons and Jason David Gibbons, will you marry me?"

Jason pulled away from his mother's side and flung his arms around Brad's neck. "Yes!"

Brad wrapped his arms around the little boy but remained on bended knee. "Hope?"

She batted back the tears of joy. Maybe sometimes fairy tales really did come true. "When it's right, it just is."

MEET CHRIS

Author of dozens of contemporary novels, including the award winning Aloha Series, Chris Keniston lives in suburban Dallas with her husband, two human children, and two canine children. Though she loves her puppies equally, she admits being especially attached to her German Shepherd rescue. After all, even dogs deserve a happily ever after.

More on Chris and her books can be found at www.chriskeniston.com.

Follow Chris on facebook at ChrisKenistonAuthor or on twitter @ckenistonauthor.

Join Chris' newsletter! Enjoy inside peeks and photographs from Chris' world and stories. Some times she'll thank her subscribers with a free copy of a new 99 cent flirt.

Please, if you enjoyed reading Flirting With Paradise, consider helping other readers find the Aloha Romance series by taking a moment to leave a review. Reviews are a blessing to authors and readers alike. Even just a few words will do! Thank you.